ANDREA CARTER AND THE

*San Francisco*
*Smugglers*

## The Circle C Adventures Series

# HOWDY!

Welcome to the Circle C. My name is Andi Carter. If you are a new reader, here's a quick roundup of my family, friends, and adventures:

I'm a tomboy who lives on a huge cattle ranch near Fresno, California, in the exciting 1880s. I would rather ride my palomino mare, Taffy, than do anything else. I mean well, but trouble just seems to follow me around.

Our family includes my mother Elizabeth, my ladylike older sister Melinda, and my three older brothers: Justin (a lawyer), Chad, and Mitch. I love them, but sometimes they treat me like a pest. My father was killed in a ranch accident a few years ago.

In **Long Ride Home**, Taffy is stolen and it's my fault. I set out to find my horse and end up far from home and in a heap of trouble.

In **Dangerous Decision**, I nearly trample my new teacher in a horse race with my friend Cory. Later, I have to make a life-or-death choice.

Next, I discover I'm the only one who doesn't know the Carter **Family Secret**, and it turns my world upside down.

In **San Francisco Smugglers**, a flood sends me to school in the city for two months. My new roommate, Jenny, and I discover that the little Chinese servant-girl in our school is really a slave.

**Trouble with Treasure** is what Jenny, Cory, and I find when we head into the mountains with Mitch to pan for gold.

And now I may lose my beloved horse, Taffy, if I tell what I saw in **Price of Truth**.

So saddle up and ride into my latest adventure!

Andi

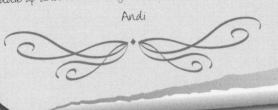

# ANDREA CARTER AND THE

# San Francisco Smugglers

## Susan K. Marlow

Kregel
Publications

*Andrea Carter and the San Francisco Smugglers*

© 2008 by Susan K. Marlow

Published by Kregel Publications, a division of Kregel, Inc., P.O. Box 2607, Grand Rapids, MI 49501.

ISBN 978-0-8254-3446-4

Printed in the United States of America

10 11 12 13 14 / 6 5 4 3 2

For Jesus Christ,
the Author behind the author,
without whom this story could not
have been written.

## Chapter One

# THE FLOOD

F lood's a comin'!"

Andi Carter jerked her head up from where she slumped, chin in hands, daydreaming. *A flood? Now? In the middle of church?* She straightened in her seat and watched a man wearing a rain slicker pound his way to the front of the sanctuary and steady himself against the pulpit.

Andi's brother Chad leaped to his feet. "Where, Fred?"

"From the east. We need every man to lend a hand with the levees, or the water will take most of the town."

"What about teams with plows to cut ditches?" Sam Blake shouted. "My livery was hit pretty hard a couple years back. I aim to make sure the water passes me by this time around."

Fred pushed away from the pulpit and headed back down the aisle. "The Bentley brothers are working on it; Wheeler's passin' out shovels." He paused and waved a hand in the air. "We gotta go!"

As one, the worshippers rose and began gathering up their outerwear.

Andi jumped up with the rest of her family. Her heart leaped. What luck! A flood was much better than listening to one of Reverend Harris's long, dull sermons. She'd never seen a real flood. The Circle C ranch lay more than an hour's drive from Fresno, on high ground. The yearly risk of flooding from Fancher, Red, and Big Dry creeks never threatened the Carter spread. Andi had to content herself with hearing stories of folks working together to channel the water away from their beloved town. Her friend Cory's secondhand tales were always laced with thrills and narrow escapes.

Scrambling along behind her three brothers, Andi paused at the door of the church and looked east. Nothing. No water. No flooding. No *nothing*. If it weren't for Fred Woodworth's warning, she'd think it was just another dreary, rainy February day. The downpour of a few hours ago had turned to a light drizzle. Disappointed, she watched the men hurry away.

"I gotta get my things outta the cellar," she heard a man cry from the middle of the street. "She's comin', I tell ya!" He disappeared around the corner of the church.

Andi knew that if she didn't disappear pretty quick, she'd lose her chance to see something interesting. She glanced over her shoulder. Her mother and her older sister Melinda were busy helping the women collect their children. Melinda held a sobbing little girl, while Elizabeth Carter had her arms around a young mother. "I can't go home," Andi heard the frightened lady confess. "I couldn't stand seein' our furniture floatin' away."

Elizabeth murmured something Andi couldn't hear and led the woman toward a pew. She seemed to have forgotten about her youngest daughter.

Andi clattered down the steps and into the street. She would take a quick peek and come right back to help.

"Andi!" Cory Blake ran up beside her. His blue eyes and disheveled hair reflected his excitement. "Water's rising fast a few blocks over. If you want to see it, come with me." He grabbed her sleeve.

Without a backward glance, Andi allowed Cory to pull her along.

When they reached Tulare Street, they could go no farther. As far as Andi could see, a torrent of water was pouring down the street. She gasped. "How can a few levees and ditches control *this*?"

"You'll see. Everybody pitches in. You've never seen such shovelin' and plowin' and shoutin' and"—he grinned—"high spirits, even. No pesky flood's gonna get *us* down."

Careful to avoid the worst of the muddy stream, Cory and Andi picked their way along the raised wooden sidewalk. The water rose steadily.

One block over, men with plows and teams of horses frantically worked to channel the flood away from the business district. Cory grabbed Andi's arm and pointed toward a house surrounded by water up to its porch. "Look at Mr. Fuller."

The old man was fishing his stove wood out of the "ocean" swirling around his doorway. "Need some help?" Cory called. He waded through the churning, muddy stream and went after the floating logs. Laughing and splashing, he steered them toward Mr. Fuller's front porch. Andi stayed put and watched.

"Thanks, young fella," Mr. Fuller said. He stashed the wood safely above water.

"You look like you're enjoying this," Andi remarked when Cory sloshed his way back to higher ground. "What if the water gets deeper?"

"Then I'll get me a rowboat. It'd be fun to row around town and rescue folks. And if I couldn't find any people to rescue, I'd save chickens or cats or any poor critter caught in a fix." He tugged on her sleeve again. "If we climb to the roof of the Grand Central, we'll see everything." He didn't seem to care that he was soaked to the skin.

"No, I've seen enough. I better get back to the church. Mother doesn't know I left."

Cory shook his head. "Too late, Andi. Look."

Andi's heart sank. The flooded street had cut off the two explorers from the rest of town. She followed her friend the last couple of blocks to the railroad depot. Everywhere she looked men were building levees and cutting channels to divert the water. The clanging of shovels could hardly be heard over the rushing water, the boisterous laughter, and the shouting of orders. Andi could tell by the way the townsfolk were working together that they'd done this before. It was surely only a matter of time before Fresno returned to normal.

Suddenly she heard a yell above the clamor. "The levee broke! Water's comin' through!"

The muddy current rushed down the street and alongside the railroad embankment like a young Mississippi River. With a yelp, Cory snatched Andi's hand and yanked. "Hurry!"

They scrambled up the sloping mound of dirt and gravel, where the train tracks sat above the valley floor. With a final jerk, Cory pulled Andi to her feet. She stumbled and crashed into a cluster of Chinese residents. "Sorry," she said, righting herself.

The Chinese men ignored her. They stood silently, watching the rising floodwaters. So far, the high railroad bed had kept the flood away from the Chinatown side of the tracks—a perfect dam. But the embankment was now throwing the water back against Fresno in fresh waves.

"I think we're stuck here," Andi said.

"Stuck is right," Cory agreed. "Who knows how long it'll take before the water finally runs off?" He lowered himself to the tracks and settled down to wait.

Andi didn't feel like joining him on the soggy ground. "If it gets much higher, we're going to get soaked."

Cory cocked his head to look at her. "Andi, we already *are* soaked."

Andi shrugged. The rain had stopped for the moment, but it was damp and chilly. From the top of the roadbed, she could see the sheet of water spreading north. If the townsfolk didn't do something pretty soon, the entire town would be immersed in waist-high water, and every building filled with squishy mud.

Standing in the cold, watching the water drown her town, Andi lost her enthusiasm. Her brothers were no doubt building levees. Her mother and sister were busy helping others. But here she was, slogging around in the mud and trapped on the railroad bed until the water receded. *A flood's no fun*, she decided. *It's just a lot of hard work. I wish I was back at the church, warm and dry, helping Mother.*

Thinking about her mother made Andi glance down at her clothes. Her skirt peeked out from under her coat and clung to her legs in limp, soggy folds. Mud caked her Sunday slippers. "Mother's going to have a conniption fit. What was I thinking?" It was one thing to wade in the creek on a summer's day wearing overalls, but another thing entirely to tramp around in a February flood, dressed in her best.

"Did you say something?" Cory asked. He looked perfectly content sitting on the tracks, watching. His straw-colored hair was plastered to his head in long, dirty hanks. Mud speckled his face.

Andi didn't answer. She turned her gaze toward Chinatown. She almost envied the Chinese. Their section of town was dry. Dozens of residents, however, held shovels in their hands and wore bleak expressions. *Why?* She became more confused when a handful of shy Chinese women, with small children clinging to their blue cotton trousers, made their way to the top of the embankment. They stood off by themselves in a small, tight group.

Andi stared at them. She knew it was rude, but she couldn't help it. She had never seen a Chinese woman or girl before. There were plenty of Chinese men in Fresno, and she knew the laundryman's son, Chen Lu, by name. But the few Chinese women in town kept themselves hidden away.

A few years ago, Andi had asked her lawyer-brother, Justin, why she never saw Chen Lu in school. Justin had explained that the law in California did not allow Chinese children to attend. Andi had thought this horribly unfair. She wished there were a law forbidding *her* to go to school. Justin had laughed and sent her on her way.

Now she wondered if one of these tiny, timid women was Chen Lu's mother. She smiled tentatively at the group, but the women gathered their children closer and turned their eyes to the ground.

Suddenly, a string of high, agitated Chinese voices rose above the sound of the water. The men pointed and shouted, then began scurrying away. Andi turned to see what had upset them. A crowd of townsmen was gathering near the water tower.

Cory jumped up. "I wonder what they're up to."

"We're cutting through the embankment just north of the tower," a dirt-splattered young man told them in passing. "It's the only way we can keep the town from washing away."

Andi now realized why the Chinese men had rushed off in such a hurry. "But if they do that, Chinatown will be flooded."

The man slung his shovel over his shoulder and grinned. "Better them than us." He hurried off to help.

Andi glanced back at the bedraggled group of Chinese women and children. Would their men be able to raise levees in time to save their small community? She hoped so. She had a sad, strange feeling that the citizens of Fresno would not go out of their way to lend a hand to their neighbors on the other side of the tracks.

"I'm wet and cold," Andi said. "I want to go home."

Cory laughed. "You gonna swim?"

"I don't have to. Look." She pointed to a small boat coming toward them.

An older man with an unkempt, graying beard and worn overalls cupped his hands to his mouth and called from the boat, "Howdy, kids."

"Howdy, Mr. Henderson," Cory yelled. "Howdy, Reed."

Reed lifted an oar in greeting. "Give us a hand, would you?"

Cory and Andi snagged the prow as the rowboat scraped against the roadbed.

Mr. Henderson squinted at Andi. "Your ma's a mite worried, Andi. She wants to get back to the ranch before things get worse. She sent me to look for you. Climb aboard and I'll row you to dry land."

Andi didn't hesitate. *A mite worried? More like a mite angry, I bet.* She reached for Reed's outstretched hand.

"Careful, Andi," he warned.

Too late. Andi stepped into the small rowboat with one foot, but her mud-caked slipper slid forward. With a splash, she toppled into the floodwaters.

"I've got you!" Reed hollered. He locked a hand around her wrist and held on.

The water wasn't deep, but it was cold. Andi grabbed the edge of the boat with her free hand. Mr. Henderson dug the oars against the current, while Cory kept a firm grip on the bow.

Reed hauled Andi over the edge and dropped her into the boat. Then Cory jumped in. They drifted with the current along Front Street.

"That was close," Cory said. He'd lost his usual grin.

"Yep," Reed agreed. "The last lady we rescued fell overboard too. She swallowed so much water we had to fetch Doc Weaver." He turned to Andi. "You all right?"

Teeth chattering, Andi huddled in the bottom of the boat. "I'm fine." She wouldn't admit to the Hendersons—or to Cory—how scared she'd been when she hit the water. She hadn't been in any real danger, but she couldn't help remembering her plunge into an overflowing creek just a couple of months before. She'd almost drowned that day, and this dunking brought the terror back in full force. She closed her eyes and clenched her jaw. *I will not cry!*

Mr. Henderson's sympathetic voice brought her back to the present. "I'm right sorry, Andi. We'll have you to shore in no time."

Before long the rowboat scraped bottom. Andi and Cory climbed out onto a street away from the worst of the damage.

Mr. Henderson shook his head. "You two look like a couple of drowned rats, I'm sorry to say. Better hurry home, before you catch your death."

"Yes, s-sir. Thank you, s-sir," Andi said between chattering teeth.

"I'd best find my pa," Cory added.

Andi waved to her rescuer then turned and ran back the way she'd come. When she rounded the corner to the church, she saw her mother standing in the muddy street, near the family carriage. She was gazing toward the flooded parts of town. When she saw Andi, she shook her head.

Andi took a deep breath and hurried over. "I'm sorry, Mother. I didn't mean t—"

"Get in the carriage," Mother said.

Andi gulped and obeyed.

*I am in a heap of trouble. Again.*

*Chapter Two*

# OUT OF THE FRYING PAN . . .

A ndi blinked back tears as she sat, shivering with cold, during the hour-long ride to the Circle C. The eerie silence—broken only by the steady clop-clop of the horses' hooves and the jingling of the harness—gave Andi plenty of time to think about her foolishness. This was no doubt what her mother had in mind. But it was hard to think clearly with soggy hair and icy feet, bundled up in a lap robe.

To keep her mind off her misery, she tried conversation. "Reed Henderson fished me out of the water, Melinda. He's real nice. You should go with him instead of that ol' sourpuss, Jeffrey Sullivan."

Melinda rolled her eyes and sighed.

"Did you know they're cutting through the track bed and letting the water flood Chinatown?" When no one replied, Andi continued, "Don't you think that's a terrible idea?"

After her third and fourth attempts at conversation died, Andi was forced to admit she was in disgrace and settled back to endure the rest of the trip home in silence.

"You're home!" Andi shouted when she saw her brothers ride into the yard three days later. She slid from her palomino's back and raced to meet them. "What happened? Is the town still there? Is the water gone?"

Chad brushed Andi's words away with a tired hand and nearly

fell from his horse. "Yeah, the town's still there, but you might not recognize it." He tossed his reins at a ranch hand, who snatched them up and led the horse toward the barn. "Have Brett or Jon return these mounts to the livery later today, will you?" Chad called after him.

"*Sí, señor,*" came the cheerful reply.

"I've got some bad news for you, Andi," Mitch said.

Andi felt herself grow pale. "Did somebody drown? Did one of my friends get hurt?"

"No, nothing like that." He sighed. "I'm sorry to tell you this, sis, but the worst-hit building in town is the schoolhouse. It's still surrounded by water."

Andi frowned in confusion. This was *bad* news?

"The whole first floor is covered in a foot-deep layer of mud," Justin put in. He headed for the house. Andi trailed along, trying to make sense of her brothers' words. "Everything in Miss Hall's classroom is a loss. Your classroom upstairs escaped damage, but it's going to take weeks to put everything back in order."

"Weeks?" Andi pondered. The main floor of the building full of mud; school supplies for the little children a loss; repairs taking weeks. "Does this mean . . . ?" She held her breath.

Mitch's blue eyes twinkled. "I think so."

"We called a hasty board meeting and decided to close school for the rest of the term," Justin said. "Hopefully, we can get the building cleaned up in time to open for the spring session."

"Yippee!" Andi threw her arms around her oldest brother and hugged him tight. She was glad he was on the school board. She was probably the first kid in the county to hear the glorious news: *no school for two months!*

Her thoughts whirled with possibilities. It was only mid-February, but the days were already growing warmer. In no time, the sun would shine more often, the fruit trees begin to bud, and the meadows burst into wildflowers. For once, she'd have all day—every day—to ride Taffy and welcome spring back to the Valley and the surrounding hills.

"Thank you, Justin." She squeezed him tighter and smiled up into his face. "You're the best brother in the whole world to close school like this."

Mitch laughed. "I figured the news would hit you hard." He yanked on her braid in passing and took the steps leading to the veranda in one long stride. He eyed Chad and pulled a coin from the pocket of his muddy trousers. "I'll toss you for the tub."

"Nuthin' doin'," Chad retorted, suddenly wide awake. Then he was off, slamming through the door like a small child, with Mitch only a few steps behind.

Andi watched them go and turned to Justin. "I wonder who'll win."

"The way those two are tearing through the house, neither one will win. When Luisa gets finished with them, I'll wager they end up using the horse trough to cool their heels." Justin smiled. "I believe that will give me all the time I need for a good, long soak in the tub."

Andi laughed. Her brother was right. The Carters' fiery little Mexican housekeeper put up with no nonsense. She was just as likely to scold grown men like Chad and Mitch as she was to give Andi a piece of her mind for sliding down the banister railing. It was never a good idea to cross Luisa.

Supper that night was a gala affair for Andi. Nothing could dampen her spirits. "No school, no school," she chanted quietly while she scooped two huge spoonfuls of mashed potatoes onto her plate. *Tomorrow morning, first thing, I'll brush Taffy 'til she shines and then off we go.* She hummed and passed the potatoes to her sister.

"Your sulky mood didn't last long," Melinda said as she took the bowl from Andi's hands. "I thought the scolding and chores Mother gave you would last longer than a few days."

Although Elizabeth Carter had kept quiet during the ride home, she'd had plenty to say later. Andi found herself saddled with the job of thoroughly washing and ironing her Sunday clothes, scrubbing her slippers, and cleaning her coat. Andi had indeed felt grumpy—until this afternoon. Now nothing could dim her joy.

She elbowed her sister. "Hush. I want to hear what the boys are saying."

Flood stories dominated the supper conversation. Andi listened, wide-eyed, to the account of what had happened to Fresno after she'd left. The railroad bed had been cut, and the water began to recede shortly afterward.

"The water poured into Chinatown, didn't it?" Andi said.

Justin nodded. "I'm afraid so. But don't worry. Chinatown turned out in full force to save their quarter. They built a levee, and most of their property was spared. Which is more than I can say for the business section of Fresno."

"We battled those levees for three straight days," Chad grumbled. "They're still not secure. The banks are soft and seeping considerable water. If folks let their guard down, the levees will break, and we'll have another nice mess on our hands."

Andi put down her fork. "Justin, may I ride into town with you and see it?"

"You'll get a chance to see Fresno soon enough, Andrea," Elizabeth said from the head of the table. She took a sip of water. "The school's closing has prompted me to consider other options."

Andi swallowed. "Other options? Other options for what?"

"For your schooling."

Silence. Then, "I reckon I'm on holiday for a couple of months, Mother."

"You reckoned wrong," her mother replied. "This is an excellent opportunity to continue your education in San Francisco. You have a standing invitation to stay with Aunt Rebecca and attend Miss Whitaker's Academy for Young Ladies. I've never consented because I knew you didn't want to be away from the ranch for so long. Now we have the perfect compromise. You can finish out the winter term with Aunt Rebecca. She'll be so pleased. I'll wire her first thing in the morning to expect you this weekend—in time to begin school next Monday."

So far, Andi had not interrupted, but only because she was numb with shock. She glanced around the table and waited for somebody to jump in and say this was a bad idea. When no one came to her rescue, she shoved back her chair and leaped to her feet.

"Mother, I can't go to San Francisco. I'd simply die. Aunt Rebecca is no more than a jailer. She'll hover over me morning, noon, and night. I might as well be—"

"That's enough, Andrea," Elizabeth warned. "Sit down and finish your supper."

Andi sat. But she didn't finish her meal. Hot tears rose and threatened to spill over. Her throat swelled. She couldn't eat. Even the smell of hot apple cobbler didn't revive her appetite. She clutched her linen napkin in her lap and stared at her now-cold slab of beef and half-eaten potatoes.

After a few minutes of awkward silence, supper conversation resumed. Andi's brothers told more flood stories and discussed the plans for cleaning up Fresno. They shared the town's ideas to help folks who were temporarily homeless because of ruined furnishings and a layer of mud in their parlors.

Andi decided she'd heard enough. She could not choke down another bite of food, and flood news was suddenly unbearable. While all her friends enjoyed an unexpected holiday or pitched in to help clean up Fresno, she would be stuck nearly two hundred miles away at some fancy school for young ladies. Worse, when she wasn't in school, Aunt Rebecca would be breathing down her neck to conduct herself properly every waking moment.

Even before Andi's father was killed almost seven years ago, his older spinster sister had considered it her Christian duty to interfere with his family. Since James Carter's death, Rebecca had poked her nose in more often. Her unwavering, outdated opinions—freely aired—along with a keen sense of what was proper before God and society, made Aunt Rebecca's visits to the Circle C unbearable for Andi.

"Andrea."

Her mother's voice jerked Andi from her musing. She looked up.

"Sulking is unseemly."

"Yes, ma'am."

"I know you'd rather stay here, sweetheart. But think of Aunt Rebecca. She loves you and wants to see you. You're old enough to put aside what you want and think of an old woman." Elizabeth smiled. "And consider this: Katherine lives with Rebecca. The children, also. I don't think a visit to San Francisco will be as bad as you imagine. You've told me more than once the past month how much you miss your nieces and nephew."

Andi let out a long, slow breath. It was true she missed Levi, Betsy, and Hannah. When her sister's family had boarded the train two months ago, she'd as much as promised Levi she'd come to San Francisco to see him.

Besides, Andi knew her mother wouldn't budge once she'd made up her mind, especially if she felt it was the right thing to do. Andi shivered. The last time she had heard her family talking about a visit to Aunt Rebecca's—nearly a year ago—she'd bolted, running away with her beloved horse, Taffy. That adventure had cost her dearly. However, she'd learned something from almost losing Taffy, and she didn't want to repeat past mistakes.

"All right, Mother," she said. "I'll go."

*Chapter Three*

# . . . INTO THE FIRE

A ndi stood with her nose pressed against the window of the westbound passenger car and sighed—loudly. She watched the telegraph poles flash by and listened to the clickety-clack of the train's wheels along the track. *Can't go back, can't go back*, the wheels mocked. The landscape rushed past. She sighed again.

Justin turned a page of the newspaper he was reading. "Sigh as much as you like," he said without looking up, "but please do so while seated."

Andi slumped into the plush, red velvet seat next to her brother and scratched at the hot, sticky black stockings under her traveling skirt. When had a week flown by so fast? Within three days of Andi's agreeing to go to San Francisco, Aunt Rebecca had been wired, train tickets purchased, and luggage packed. Andi barely had time to catch her breath or say good-bye to Taffy.

The thought of being separated from her palomino mare for two whole months brought a lump to her throat. "I've changed my mind. I want to go home."

Justin lowered his paper and looked at her. "It's too late for that, so you may as well make the best of it."

"But my horse! Taffy will forget me. I miss her already. You could change Mother's mind. You can practically talk a fence post out of the ground. Mother listens to you."

"It's true I occasionally come to your rescue," Justin admitted. He laid the newspaper aside and gave Andi his full attention. "But I'm certainly not going to go up against Mother when her mind's made up. This is important to her. You can please her by attending school in the city for two months and by doing your best not to antagonize your teachers. Our sisters managed it. You can too."

"Kate and Melinda are different. They like San Francisco."

"You might grow to appreciate it as well."

Andi knew Justin was trying his best to soften what was beginning to feel more and more like a prison term. She pulled at the hot, heavy skirt and hoped the uniforms at the school were cooler than this awkward thing.

"You don't have to board at the school," Justin continued. "You're staying with Kate and the kids. The time will go by quickly. Before you know it, you'll be home." He grinned. "And think of all the chores you'll be missing."

Andi made a face. "I'd much rather muck out the barn than sit around embroidering samplers. I'm terrible at it, no matter how often Mother and Melinda have tried to teach me. I can't sit still long enough to make it come out right. And . . . and . . . Miss Whitaker will think Mother hasn't raised me properly and . . ." She flushed to think that her lack of skill in this area would reflect poorly on her mother.

Justin reached over and squeezed her hand. "Don't worry about Mother's reputation, honey. She knows there are more important things to learn than sewing a perfect seam or knowing how to serve tea. If you remember the things that really matter—like honesty, kindness, and thinking of others—then Miss Whitaker's should hold no worries for you. You certainly won't disgrace the family name, no matter *how* crooked you sew."

Andi nodded, but there wasn't time to say anything more. Justin was pointing out the window. "Take a look. We're coming into Oakland. We'll catch the ferry, cross the bay, and then we'll be in San Francisco."

Andi glanced out the window. Neither Oakland nor San Francisco held any charms for her. They were just two big cities next to a lot of water. She waited silently as the train puffed and jerked its way into the depot.

The ferry trip across the dull, gray waters of San Francisco Bay did a fine job of reflecting Andi's dreary mood. A chill breeze whipped across her face; a wave leaped up and sprayed icy water against her cheeks. She shivered and pulled her cloak tighter around her shoulders. She didn't like all this water. It looked deep. And dark. She reached out and grasped Justin's hand.

He looked at her in surprise, then seemed to know how she felt. "If you think the bay looks big, wait 'til you see the ocean."

"I don't intend to."

The closer the ferry chugged to the city, the taller and more threatening the buildings appeared. Andi had seen San Francisco once or twice when she was younger, but she didn't remember the buildings looking so tall—or that there were so many of them.

The ferry blew its long, low whistle and began to slow down. White, foaming water churned up all around the ship, and Andi gripped the railing to catch her balance. "Give me the mountains. The city folks can keep all this water."

Justin laughed.

The first thing that struck Andi when she stepped off the ferry was the noise and the feverish activity. Everybody seemed to be in a tremendous hurry, and they didn't hurry quietly. Swarms of vehicles, from pushcarts to carriages, rattled along the streets. Peddlers with trays of flowers, neckties, penknives, and buttons threaded their way through the crush of people, yelling the advantages of their wares. Andi stayed close to Justin while he hired a rig and made arrangements to have the baggage loaded. Then they climbed inside.

As Justin gave the driver instructions, Andi noticed how easily her brother slipped into the pace of the city. He looked perfectly at ease—confident and comfortable with the hustle and bustle of the largest city on the west coast. Andi could tell that Justin liked San Francisco. He liked it a lot. He was smiling.

The horse's hooves clattered noisily along the cobbled streets. The sound added to the clanging of a cable car climbing a steep hill. Andi poked her head out the window and craned her neck to see the top. A long way up, she decided. Perhaps she might—just might—take one ride on a cable car.

Quite a few blocks later, at the top of another hill, the coach stopped in front of an enormous Victorian home. Bay windows and balconies stuck out all over the house. Pillars supported a large veranda. Andi recognized it at once as Aunt Rebecca's home. Her heart sank at the thought of staying here for two months.

A high squeal broke into Andi's thoughts. "They're here, Mama!"

Instantly Andi forgot about Aunt Rebecca. She flung the cab door open, jumped down, and hurried across the sidewalk. "Betsy!" She opened her arms and her six-year-old niece flew into them. Ten-year-old Levi slammed the wrought-iron gate aside and ran over. Little Hannah scampered across the yard to greet her. "I've missed you so much," Andi said with a grin.

"I missed you too," Betsy said. "How's my pony? And the kittens? Are they bigger?"

"Nearly big enough to have their own kittens."

"What about Patches?" Levi broke in.

"He's out on the range, but Mitch says he's yours next time you visit."

"Nandi," Hannah said, yanking on Andi's skirt, "I'm fwree-and-a-half." She held up four fingers.

Andi laughed. "You're getting big." She looked at Levi and the girls. They looked the same, yet different. What was it? Suddenly she knew. "You look mighty fine in those new clothes."

Levi scowled. "Auntie made us get slicked up to meet you. I told her you wouldn't recognize us in these fancy duds, but you don't argue with Auntie." He sighed. "At least not much."

Betsy twirled around. "I like wearing pretty things. I'm learning to dance. Someday I'll be a . . . a . . ."

"Debutante," a cheerful voice finished for her. Katherine pulled Andi into a hug. "It's nice to see you, little sister." Then she hugged Justin. "Good trip?"

He flicked a glance at Andi. "It could have been better."

Andi chose to ignore the remark.

The driver unloaded Andi's satchel and two carpetbags, accepted payment from Justin, and touched the brim of his cap. As the rig clattered down the street, Andi heard a new voice.

"What are you doing, standing around outside? Goodness! It's starting to rain again. A grayer, wetter winter in this city I've never known, and I've seen my share of them." Aunt Rebecca paused for a quick breath before continuing. "Stay away from the street, Levi. Justin, there's no need to bother with the luggage. Thomas will see to your things. Come along, out of this miserable weather. Hurry inside."

Andi marveled at Aunt Rebecca's ability to carry on two or three conversations at one time. She ordered her servants to see to the bags, instructed a maid to prepare the parlor for afternoon tea, scolded Levi for swinging on the gate, and asked Kate to check with the house-keeper to make sure Andi's room had been aired.

Neither Kate nor the children seemed ill at ease with their aunt's manner. Hannah sucked her thumb and clung to Andi's skirt while Betsy held Andi's hand, clearly happy to be with her again. Levi ignored his aunt, swung on the gate one more time, and dashed inside the house just before the door closed.

Aunt Rebecca turned to Andi. "I'm pleased to see you're finally here, although it took a flood to bring it to pass." She pursed her lips. "I've enrolled you in the academy. You commence school Monday morning. Edith Whitaker and I are dear friends. She's looking forward to meeting you and furthering your education."

Andi opened her mouth to say "yes, ma'am" but Aunt Rebecca wasn't finished.

"I am on the board—a founding member, you know—and I expect great things from you, my dear. Oh, if only James had lived to see this day. All three of his girls educated at the academy." She paused and took a delicate, lacy handkerchief from her sleeve and wiped her eyes. Then she reached out and pulled Andi to her ample bosom. Just as quickly, she straightened. "Go to your room, Andrea, and freshen up for tea. Margarita will show you where it is."

"I can show her, Auntie," Betsy piped up. "Let me. Please let me!"

"You may go along, Elizabeth, but Margarita will show her." She turned to Andi. "She will help you dress and tend to your needs."

Margarita, a pretty, petite Spanish girl no older than Melinda, curtsied to Andi and started up the stairs.

Andi looked helplessly at Justin. She neither wanted nor needed a personal maid. Aunt Rebecca's domineering personality and nonstop talking made Andi feel more trapped than ever.

"I'll see you at tea, Andi," Justin said with a grin, and followed Aunt Rebecca down the hallway.

"Please, Justin," Andi pleaded that evening before bed. "You can't leave me here. You simply *can't*. I'll go mad—*loco* as Crazy Billy—if I stay here."

Justin folded his arms across his chest and leaned against the doorframe. "I doubt that. I can't see you running through the streets of San Francisco in your underclothes the way Crazy Billy likes to run through Fresno in his long johns. For one thing, it's much too cold this time of year." He chuckled.

Andi collapsed onto her bed. "That's not funny." She gave her brother a pleading look. "Can't you at least stay over Sunday and take me to school on Monday?"

Justin shook his head. "I've got to be in Sacramento first thing Monday morning." He held up a hand when Andi started to protest. "I promise I'll stop by whenever I'm in San Francisco."

"But Justin . . ."

"No buts. Aunt Rebecca is near bursting with pride to take you to school. Humor her, Andi. Bite your tongue when she gushes and hold your temper when she makes demands."

"How am I going to do that, big brother?"

"With prayer, honey. A lot of prayer." Justin crossed the room, leaned over, and planted a kiss on Andi's forehead. "Now, good night."

*Chapter Four*

# MISS WHITAKER'S ACADEMY

T his is a *school?*" Andi pulled herself from the carriage and stared. "It looks like some old mansion." She and Aunt Rebecca had ridden up and down hills, around corners, and past a streetcar until Andi was so turned around she knew she'd never find her way back to her aunt's. The houses lining both sides of the street were huge, rambling monstrosities. Andi found it hard to believe this would be her schoolhouse for the next two months.

"It *was* a mansion," Aunt Rebecca explained, "built during the gold rush by someone who struck it rich. Much like your father did when he became wealthy from his prospecting and built his first home not too far from here." She shook her gray head. "'Tis a pity he didn't take to city life instead of pouring the rest of his fortune into that . . . that . . ."

"Ranch," Andi finished. If Aunt Rebecca was sorry Father had relocated to the Valley all those years ago, Andi certainly wasn't.

Rebecca stepped out of the carriage and gave Andi a piercing look. "This place was sold, remodeled, and expanded over the years into Miss Whitaker's Academy. It is situated among the most prestigious homes in San Francisco, you know."

Andi looked at her blankly.

"Nob Hill, my dear. A block or two higher and you will be at the top, among the cream of San Francisco's finest families."

Andi followed her aunt's gaze. The houses all looked alike to her. She turned around and glanced down the wide, steep street. "What's way down there?"

Aunt Rebecca's look turned grim. "Chinatown—and worse."

*Chinatown!* That sounded much more interesting. Andi shaded her eyes to get a better look. "Do you suppose we—?"

"Stay away from Chinatown," her aunt warned. "A yellow hand will reach out and grab you. Or a trap door will open and swallow you up. A dark, dangerous place, that Chinatown."

"But—"

"Merciful heavens, child! No more questions." Rebecca impatiently hurried her toward the wide gate in front of the school and continued her recitation of the merits of Miss Whitaker's Academy. "I think you'll be surprised at how spacious the school and grounds are. The girls find plenty of room for walking and playing croquet in their free hours. You'll see lovely gardens and a fountain. The school also stables a few horses for riding lessons and—"

"Do you think I might be able to ride?" Andi blurted. "Oh, I'm sorry for interrupting, but may I?"

Rebecca pursed her lips in an expression Andi had come to recognize as her disapproving gaze. Levi had half-warned, half-joked about it yesterday. "Watch out for Auntie's sourpuss look. It means she's getting ready to scold you. Most times you won't be sure about what."

"The grounds are not *that* extensive, my dear. The academy's horses are for the carriages and for young ladies receiving lessons in horsemanship. This is a city of cobblestones and culture, not thousands of acres of nothing. You will not be permitted to jump on a horse and ride wherever and whenever you want, as you are allowed to do at home. Do you understand?"

Downcast, Andi nodded. *What am I going to do for two months without riding?*

"Good," Rebecca said. "Leisurely riding excursions in Golden Gate Park are the order of the day, not the wild, devil-may-care riding to which you are accustomed."

"So I *will* get to ride?"

Rebecca sighed. "Yes. But I daresay your time will be well spent correcting any poor horsemanship habits you have picked up on the ranch." She unlatched the gate into the school grounds. "Now come along."

The grounds were well tended. A clipped lawn and hedges bordered the walkway up to the immense front porch. A few winter-hardy flowers dotted the gardens with splashes of color. Eucalyptus trees shaded the school on three sides. Andi decided it wasn't a bad-looking place, after all.

Rebecca climbed the stairs to the gabled porch and rang the bell. Andi watched through the stained-glass window beside the door as a starched, uniformed maid scurried to answer. She opened the double doors and admitted them into a huge entrance hall. A wide staircase wound its way along both sides of the foyer, meeting at the second floor in a long balcony that overlooked the entryway.

Andi's mouth fell open.

"Good morning, Miss Carter." The maid dropped a curtsy. Her tight black curls bounced under her cap as she nodded to Andi. "'Mornin', miss." Another curtsy.

"Good morning, Celia," Aunt Rebecca said.

Andi gave Celia a tiny smile.

"Miss Whitaker is waiting to see you," Celia said, "if you'll please follow me." She led them down a long, paneled hallway to the last door on the right and knocked.

"Enter," a crisp voice answered.

Celia ushered them into the headmistress's office. "Miss Carter, ma'am."

"Thank you, Celia. That will be all."

Andi made a long, slow sweep of the room. It was part library, part parlor. Behind Miss Whitaker's desk, two enormous windows opened onto a breathtaking view of the surrounding area. San Francisco stretched out below Andi's eyes in all directions, ending in the shining expanse of the bay. As she watched, silent fingers of curling gray fog began to billow up and sift through the streets, cloaking the buildings.

Miss Whitaker's low, scratchy voice yanked Andi from the mesmerizing view outside. "Good morning, Rebecca. So nice to see you." She rose from behind her immense mahogany desk and squeezed Rebecca's hand.

"And you, Edith," Rebecca replied. Then she smiled. "This is my niece, Andrea."

Miss Whitaker peered at her newest student through a pair of spectacles perched on the end of her long, thin nose. "Welcome to our academy, Andrea. I knew your sisters. Delightful girls."

Andi curtsied. "Thank you." She watched as Miss Whitaker returned to her seat. The woman reminded her of Mrs. Evans, the undertaker's wife: small, bony, brown hair, dark eyes and . . . *quick to holler at you for running through her flowerbed or for making too much noise passing by her house,* Andi thought in dismay.

Rebecca took her seat across the desk from the headmistress and waved Andi into a straight-back chair beside her. "I want it understood, Edith, that my niece is to be treated like any other young lady here. No special favors."

"Of course, Rebecca. There's no place for mollycoddling at this academy."

"Thomas will be bringing her things directly, so she can settle in before nightfall," Rebecca continued.

Aunt Rebecca's comment brought Andi up short. She pulled her gaze from the cheerful, crackling fire in the fireplace across the room and blurted, "What about my things?"

Miss Whitaker looked at Andi with disapproval. "You have no business interrupting a conversation between your elders."

Andi reddened. "I beg your pardon, Miss Whitaker. I only wanted to know what Aunt Rebecca meant when she said Thomas would be dropping my things by."

Rebecca raised her hand. "It's all right, Edith." She turned to

Andi. "You are boarding here, like the other young ladies under Miss Edith's tutelage."

"But I'm a day student. Mother said I'd be staying with you and Kate and the . . ." Her voice trailed off at the outraged expression on Miss Whitaker's face.

"The proper response is 'yes, ma'am,'" the headmistress prompted.

"Please, Aunt Rebecca," Andi pleaded, ignoring the prune-faced woman behind the desk. "I don't want to stay here."

"Miss Whitaker no longer accepts day students. She has already made an exception to take you this late in the term because you are my niece. The matter is settled."

Andi heard the warning in her aunt's voice and paused. If she talked back, Miss Whitaker would think Mother hadn't taught her any manners. For that reason—and no other—she swallowed her angry words and whispered, "Yes, ma'am." But inside she was steaming. Aunt Rebecca had not only tricked Andi, but Mother and Justin as well. *Leave it to Aunt Rebecca to have the last word.*

Clearly mollified at her niece's submission, Rebecca reached out and patted her hand. "I am doing this for your own good and for your education, my dear. You will be at an advantage, surrounded by other young ladies and having strict standards for your behavior. Once you settle in, I'm sure there will be times when you may occasionally make a brief visit to my home." She glanced at her friend. "Isn't that so, Edith?"

"Weekend privileges with family are earned." Miss Whitaker's thin lips parted in a smile that did not reach her eyes. "But I see no reason why our newest student should not enjoy such privileges."

Rebecca stood. "I must be on my way." She turned to Andi. "Good-bye, Andrea."

Resigned to her fate, Andi stood and allowed her aunt to embrace her. *It's only for two months.* "Good-bye, Aunt Rebecca."

The headmistress wasted neither time nor unnecessary words with her newest pupil. Miss Whitaker consulted a small timepiece pinned to her bodice, shook her head, and rose.

"The first class has already commenced, and I will not interrupt the lecture. You may join the other young ladies for French instruction at ten o'clock. It is the second door on the left. Until then . . ." She rang a bell. Immediately Celia appeared, as if she'd been stationed just outside, awaiting a summons. "Show Miss Carter to her room."

A few minutes later, Celia opened the door to a room tucked away in a corner on the second floor. "Here you are, miss." The maid curtsied and disappeared down the hall.

Andi pushed the door wide open and peeked at what would be her living quarters for the next two months. It was eerily silent. Andi wanted to run the other way—back to the constant clamor of a working ranch, with its familiar rustling and shouting of men at work; the rattling of wagons; the snorting of horses and the bellowing of cattle; even the sound of the occasional mishap, when Chad yelled so loud the whole ranch could hear him. She wished he were here now, yelling at *her*.

She sighed and stepped into the room, which smelled musty and stale. *Like no one really lives here*, Andi thought. She missed the scent of living things—of horses, of newly harvested alfalfa hay, and the sweat of her brothers from a long, hard day working the cattle. Even the rank odor of a stall in need of mucking out was better than this dead smell.

Andi crossed the room and flung aside the dark-blue velvet draperies. She peered through the glass and into the yard. The fog she'd seen creeping in earlier hung over the grounds in a wet, gray mist. She pressed close to the window. Was that a building behind the fog? The stable, maybe? She had an hour to fill, and anything was better than sitting alone in this cramped, stuffy room.

Andi hurried toward the door, barely taking time to notice the two neatly made beds or the simple washstand, which held a white china bowl and pitcher. A second bed probably meant a roommate, but she didn't want to think about a strange girl sharing her room. Not now. She spared no more than a passing glance at a tall wardrobe as she shut the door and headed down the hallway.

Before she'd gone a dozen steps, she discovered the servants' staircase. She knew these stairs led to the kitchen, which would certainly open onto a back porch of some kind and into the yard. She held on to the narrow railing and clattered down the steps.

Andi burst into a huge, steaming kitchen. High-pitched, piercing Chinese voices brought her to a standstill. An older Chinese man in blue cotton trousers and a loose-fitting tunic was screaming at a small girl. The child ran sobbing into a corner and cowered there. An old woman added her voice to the confusion, then reached out and yanked the girl to her feet. She delivered a sound slap that sent the child flying. Scrambling to her feet, the little girl scampered across the room and crashed into Andi, who steadied her and kept her from tumbling to the floor.

Instantly, the voices ceased. The Chinese girl, eyes huge, untangled herself from Andi's hold, backed up, and stared. Her wailing died away. The other Chinese gaped. The only sound came from the tea kettle, which whistled from the cook stove, demanding attention.

Andi's heart thumped wildly. *Poor little thing. She's not much bigger than Betsy.* "Are you all right?" she asked aloud. Although horrified at the harsh treatment she'd witnessed, a sudden, growing delight swelled inside her. She had never met a Chinese girl before, and now—right before her eyes—one had presented herself. "I'm Andi. Do you speak English?"

The old woman shot the girl a silencing look. The girl shrank back and looked at the floor, trembling. With a scowl, the man stepped forward and bowed stiffly to Andi. "What missee do here? No come into kitchen. You lost, missee?"

"I'm looking for the back door," Andi replied quickly. Obviously, she'd done something wrong. The man, while respectful, seemed very angry.

"No back door here. Kitchen no place for missee. Kitchen belong to Feng Chee. You go now."

But Andi had recovered her composure, and she was curious. "Does your little girl speak English? Do you think I could talk with her sometime?"

The Chinese man turned dark, unreadable eyes on Andi and shook his head. His pigtail whipped back and forth. "No. Much work for Lin Mei. No time play. Very busy." He scowled again. "You go now, missee. No come in kitchen. You understand?"

No, Andi did *not* understand. She wanted to talk to the Chinese girl—what was her name—Lin Mei? Faraway China seemed exotic and exciting. Why couldn't she occasionally sit at the kitchen table and visit with a real Chinese girl, maybe even drink Chinese tea and sample an Oriental treat?

But Feng Chee was adamant. "Missee go now." He pointed to a door on the other side of the kitchen. "Back door there. Stay away from kitchen of Feng Chee. You understand? Kitchen no place for—"

Andi waved his words away and started across the room. "Yes, I heard you. The kitchen's no place for me. I'm leaving." She reached the back door, flung it open, and caught Lin Mei's gaze. Andi smiled at her before stepping out into the cold, foggy San Francisco morning.

## Chapter Five

# A WHIFF OF HOME

Andi heard the horses before she saw them. The familiar whickering sounded sweet to her ears, and she broke into a run. She knew she could find the stables—fog or no fog. She was drawn to the horses like a hungry calf to its mama.

A long, low building appeared. She rounded the corner, found the wide doors, and pushed them open. Without hesitation, she entered. The rich smells of hay, saddle soap, and horses greeted her. Above the nickering of the half-dozen horses, Andi heard a lone voice pleading softly in Spanish. She hurried down the aisle and found herself outside a large box stall in the back of the stable. Inside the stall, a tall, dark young man was stroking a copper-colored mare and murmuring,

"I know you are tired, but it will soon be over. You will have a little one and it will seem as if no time has passed. Do not worry, *chiquita*. I will not leave you, but you must be patient. You must not give up. Try again, for me. For your Juan Carlos." The youth's voice dropped to a whisper, and he stroked the mare's nose.

"Is she foaling?" Andi asked. Her question needed no answer. It was clear the mare was in labor and having a rough time of it.

The youth whirled, saw Andi, and leaped to his feet. His eyes, dark and stormy at her unexpected interruption, bored into hers for an instant. Then his shoulders drooped and he dropped his gaze to the ground. "Good morning, *señorita*," he mumbled. "Forgive, please, but the English I do not speak so well."

"*No se preocupe. Yo hablo español*," Andi assured him. His head snapped up and his mouth dropped open. "My name's Andi," she continued in Spanish. She leaned over the stall's half-door for a better look. "I heard you talking to the mare. I didn't mean to interrupt, but I'm lonely. The horses drew me into the stable." She caught Juan Carlos's surprised look. Before he could say anything, she rushed on. "Please let me stay and help. I can fetch and carry things; I know how to behave around a mare during her time. I love horses, and I miss my Taffy. *¿Por favor?*"

Juan Carlos seemed to relax. He pulled at his lip, and his eyes lost their guarded look. A smile replaced his frown. "*Sí,* I would welcome your help. The stable master, *Señor* Hunter, is away and is not expected back until late tonight. Penny—this mare—is not due to foal for another week. I am alone, and I . . . I am afraid the mare will die. Then *Señor* Hunter will have me beaten."

Andi opened the door to the stall and joined Juan Carlos. "Why doesn't *Señora* Whitaker send for a veterinarian or a stockman?"

Juan lowered himself beside the mare and shook his head. "The *señora* cares little for what goes on in the stables. *Señor* Hunter, he could perhaps convince the *señora* of the need, but I am only a stable hand. She would not believe me. I fear Penny must get along without good help." He gave Andi a stricken look. "This is her first foal."

Andi recalled foaling time on the Circle C. Usually, one day she'd see fat, ungainly mares on the range and the next day the same mares with their wobbly, knobby-kneed colts and fillies frisking at their sides. Rarely did a mare need help. But when one did—day or night—Chad and Mitch went into action.

Andi squatted beside the mare and stroked her flank. "Don't worry. We won't leave you. But you've got to do this yourself." She swallowed and looked at Juan Carlos. "Sometimes when a mare takes a long time to deliver, it means the foal is stuck. When that happens, my brother reaches inside and . . . and helps sort things out. Can you do that?"

Juan grew pale, but he set his jaw. "I can if I must." Then he let out a long, slow breath. "But I hope it does not come to that. I fear I would do more harm than good."

Later, when the mare had finally dropped her foal and was cleaning him off, Andi felt relieved; she and Juan Carlos had not needed to help, after all. The colt was big—no doubt about it—but he'd come easily, once Penny had decided to get on with it. The long labor hadn't hurt either the mare or her newborn.

Andi sat in the straw, transfixed at the sight of the new family. The colt was the spitting image of his mama—bright and shiny as a new penny. Andi sighed with pleasure when the mare seemed to accept her as easily as she did Juan.

"She is honoring you with her friendship," he said with a laugh as he cleaned away the soiled straw. "That is not to be taken lightly."

"Perhaps these next two months won't be as bad as I feared," Andi replied. When Juan Carlos gave her a questioning look, Andi went on to explain how she'd come to be enrolled in Miss Whitaker's Academy for Young Ladies. "I was fixing to be horribly lonesome for my horse, Taffy, but now"—she looked at the two horses and grinned—"I think I'll be all right. You and the horses can keep me company until I return to the ranch."

Instead of agreeing, Juan Carlos looked grim. "I am afraid that will not be possible. You are a young lady enrolled in the school. I am a stable hand—a mere servant. If *Señora* Whitaker were to learn you have been friendly with me, it could cost me my job." He sighed. "I am very sorry, *señorita*."

"But back home I always follow the ranch hands around. My friend is the daughter of our cook. Her brother's your age. I talk to Joselito and Rosa all the time."

"Things are different here in San Francisco," Juan Carlos said bitterly. "I am of noble birth. My grandfather was a *don*, a respected nobleman. He owned thousands of acres—a Spanish land grant in Old California—but he lost it to the land-grabbing Americans. Now I work as a servant to the ignorant *gringos*, who treat me worse than my grandfather treated his Indian workers on his *hacienda*."

"*¡Qué triste!*" Andi said in sympathy. "How sad!"

Juan's voice lost its edge. "My grandfather and father are dead, *señorita*. This job is the only thing that keeps my mother and younger sisters fed. I must not lose it. So . . . although I thank you for your help and company today, you cannot treat me as an equal. You must go."

"We can't be friends?" The thought of being unwelcome in the stables made Andi's spirits droop.

Juan relented with a sigh. "Perhaps secretly you may visit, when you are lonely and wish to converse in the loveliest tongue on earth." He grinned, and Andi's spirits rose. "But it will be difficult. *Señor* Hunter has eyes like the hawk and a loose tongue. *Señora* Whitaker will soon learn of your visits. If you are careful and are willing to take a chance, I am willing to speak with you. But not often. And never when the other young ladies are present." He lost his smile and met her gaze like an equal. "Is this clear?" His tone was no longer that of a servant, but of the grandson of a *don*—one used to being obeyed.

Andi accepted his words without hesitation. "*Claro qué sí, Don Juan Carlos*. Of course."

A smile tugged at Juan's mouth. "*¡Vayase!* Go on with you!"

Andi left the stables with a light heart. She was already planning her next visit to Penny and her colt when the sound of scurrying feet broke into her musing.

"Missee come. Come quick." The little Chinese girl from the kitchen slid to a stop beside Andi. Her breath came in small gasps. "Please to hurry."

"Why? What's wrong?"

Lin Mei looked at Andi in desperate appeal. "Mistress look in school. Not to find you. Mistress very, very angry." She wagged her head. "Missee not have per-mis-sion"—she pronounced the long English word carefully—"to leave school. Missee has missed morning classes and"—Lin Mei clasped her hands to her small chest and gulped—"and midday meal."

Andi stopped short. The time! She glanced at the sky. The fog had lifted since her stay in the stables, and the sun stood high overhead. Lin Mei was right. She'd missed the entire first morning of classes. Miss Whitaker would indeed be angry. But oh, how much nicer it had been to watch Penny foal than to sit in a dull class of grammar or French.

Lin Mei took hold of Andi's sleeve and began to half-drag her back to the school, pleading all the time to hurry. Her words poured out in a steady stream of rapid, broken English. The headmistress, she said, was ready to send for the police, fearing Andi had been kidnapped and spirited away to the dark side of San Francisco.

By the time they finished scurrying up the walk, Andi had caught some of Lin Mei's fear. The child seemed truly concerned for Andi's welfare.

Lin Mei reached for the doorknob, but Andi held her off. "Wait," she said, stopping on the wide veranda. The little girl looked up in surprise. A large bruise darkened her cheek, where she'd been struck earlier. Her eyes were bright and wary. "Before we go inside, may I ask you something?"

The girl's gaze darted back and forth; she gave a quick nod, like a jerk.

"How long have you worked here?"

Lin Mei held up four fingers.

"Four months?" The girl shook her head. "Four years?" A nod. "But you can't be more than eight or nine years old." Another nod. "That means you started working as a servant when you were just a tiny thing." Andi was aghast. She couldn't imagine someone so young scurrying around a hot, steamy kitchen, scrubbing pans and mopping floors. It was pitiful. "Why do your parents make you work so hard?"

Lin Mei dropped her head. "You not understand, missee."

"Andi."

Lin Mei shrugged. "You not understand . . . missee . . . Andi. Feng Chee and Wen Shu not parents. They master and mistress. They buy me long time, off boat from Canton." She looked up. Two bright tears glistened in her large, brown eyes. "I *mui tsai* . . . slave."

*Chapter Six*

# NEW FRIENDS

If Lin Mei had said "I am a rattlesnake," Andi would not have been more surprised. A slave? Everybody knew slavery had been abolished sixteen years ago. But then, Lin Mei was only a little girl, and a Chinese girl at that. Perhaps she didn't know about the War Between the States.

Andi took hold of Lin Mei's shoulders and looked into her dark eyes. "There isn't any slavery," she said slowly and clearly. "We fought a war to put a stop to it. Everybody's free."

Lin Mei said nothing. She bowed her head and looked at the ground.

Andi frowned. "What's wrong?"

"Many slaves in *Kum Sum*," Lin Mei said in a quiet voice.

"*Kum Sum*?" Andi shook her head, puzzled. "What's that?"

The girl shrugged. "Here." Her arm swept the sky in a half-circle. "All this place. *Kum Sum*—Golden Mountain." She pointed beyond the school, toward the San Francisco skyline. "You go Chinatown. I show you this one or that one who is slave. Many, many girl slaves; many boats bring more. Chinatown full of slaves." She leaned closer to Andi and whispered. "And not only Chinatown. Many slaves—"

The kitchen door flew open, cutting off Lin Mei's words. Feng Chee reached out his clawlike hand and snatched her away from Andi. He gave Lin Mei a sharp slap across the face and flung her through the doorway, screaming at her the entire time. The child whimpered and scuttled away.

Andi skipped backward, out of the raging cook's path. Who knew if his next whack would be aimed at *her*? A mixture of terror and uncertainty swirled around in her empty stomach.

Feng Chee didn't hit her, but his angry words burned her ears. "What you do, missee? No talk Lin Mei, understand? Lin Mei very busy. I warn you, missee. Keep away!" He shook his fist at her, unleashed a torrent of Chinese, and disappeared behind Lin Mei. The door slammed shut, and Andi was alone.

But not for long. Around the corner of the veranda, from another entrance, the maid Celia appeared. At the sight of Andi, her dark eyes widened. "Whatever were you thinking, miss? The mistress is fit to be tied. Come along now." She led Andi past the kitchen entrance, around the porch, and entered the main part of the school. Then she stopped and looked at her. "Miss Whitaker wants to see you immediately."

In her usual, abrupt way, Miss Whitaker got straight to the point. She sat—stiff and formal—behind her mahogany desk and said, "The pupils under my care do not wander off whenever or wherever they please. We have specific times for outdoor exercise." She slid a thick sheet of cream-colored paper across the desktop. "I expect you to read and comply with the academy's rules of conduct."

Andi reluctantly picked up the paper. She didn't have to read it to know what it said. "Yes, ma'am."

"Perfect neatness in person is expected of every young lady," Miss Whitaker continued. "No romping or loud conversation, no rudeness of manner, will be allowed during the recess period." She peered at Andi over her spectacles—from the stray pieces of straw in her dark hair to her rumpled blouse and skirt. Andi knew she had failed the "perfect neatness" test already.

Miss Whitaker sighed. "Your first day, Andrea. Your very first day.

You missed French instruction and your mathematics class, as well as the midday meal."

Andi wasn't sorry she missed French and mathematics, but the grumbling of her empty stomach told her she regretted missing luncheon. "I'm sorry, Miss Whitaker. I was lonely. I found the stables, and I lost track of the time." She smiled. "Your horses are beautiful. How often do the girls ride? Do they just ride around the grounds, or do they go to the park? Is it far? I look forward to riding very much."

"Riding in Golden Gate Park is a privilege reserved for pupils who consistently turn in excellent work and exhibit behavior above reproach. I sincerely hope you will be able to join us on Sunday afternoons for this pleasure."

Andi let the words sink in. *I may have to content myself with sneaking off to visit Penny and Juan Carlos.* "I hope so too," she said aloud.

Miss Whitaker rose. "There is another matter to discuss before I show you to your afternoon classes. It has come to my attention that you passed through the kitchen today." She didn't give Andi a chance to confirm or deny it. "This is not allowed. Neither is engaging the servants in conversation. It is beneath your dignity to associate with them, and they are too busy for idle chatter."

Andi gathered her courage and said, "Did you know your cook beats the little Chinese girl who works in the kitchen? He's terribly cruel. Lin Mei is his slave."

Miss Whitaker picked up a stack of papers from her desk and headed for the door. "Lin Mei is his niece. Feng Chee took her in when her parents died of the fever a few years ago. I remember it well."

"I saw him hit her," Andi said. "She's scared to death of him. Can't you do anything to—?"

Miss Whitaker whirled on her. "Feng Chee has complete charge of the kitchen and what goes on there. It is his domain. How he manages his family is no concern of ours, Andrea. Don't be taken in by a lying little Chinese. You mind what I say and keep away from the kitchen. Is that clear?"

Andi nodded and followed the headmistress, sick at heart.

The rest of the day passed in a blur. Andi's stomach gnawed with hunger, but she refused to give in and feel sorry for herself. The hours she'd spent with Penny and Juan Carlos were worth the rumbling noises and hunger pangs. She'd skip luncheon every day if she could exchange it for an hour in the stables. *That's not likely to happen though.* She sighed and turned back to her spelling book.

Andi trudged upstairs, worn out from a long afternoon of doing nothing. Nothing interesting, anyway. She had one free hour before supper, and she knew her room needed attention. Her luggage had probably arrived. It would take most of the hour to unpack and straighten her things. She didn't intend to earn a disgrace mark for untidiness. She wanted to go riding in the park next Sunday nearly as badly as she wanted to go home. And riding in the park was a much more achievable goal.

Her hand clutched the crumpled rules of the school. She'd memorized them during Latin, the last class of the day. Latin was so dull that Andi feared she would fall asleep if she didn't do *something*. Putting the school's rules to memory wasn't a bad way to fill the time. She told herself that if following the rules and doing well in her classes allowed her to go riding, then she'd sure as shootin' do the best she could. Two months was a long time to hold a grudge against Aunt Rebecca for making her board here. If she could stay over Saturdays with Kate and the kids, and return in time to horseback ride in Golden Gate Park, it would be easier to get through the rest of the term.

When she arrived at her room, Andi found the door slightly ajar. She pushed it open and stepped through the doorway. Sure enough, her carpetbags and satchel were piled in a heap next to her bed.

But it wasn't the baggage that made her stop and stare. It was the strange girl her own age perched on the nearest bed. She sat hunched over, jabbing at a length of linen with a needle and thread. A mop of fiery-red hair cascaded around her shoulders and down her back in long, unruly tangles. A multitude of freckles covered her nose and round cheeks. Andi watched in fascination as the girl's face scrunched up with the effort of guiding the needle through the embroidery hoop.

"Who are you?" Andi asked.

With a yelp, the girl leaped from the bed. She put her finger in her mouth, sucked it, then shouted, "Don't you know better than to sneak up on a body?" She thrust her finger in Andi's face. A drop of blood oozed from the tip. "Look what you made me do! Dratted needle. Hurts like blazes."

Andi's mouth dropped open.

Suddenly, the girl's eyes widened. She scurried past Andi and slammed the door shut. Then she turned around and leaned against the door. "If Miss Whitaker catches wind of my talk, she'll give me so many disgrace marks, I'll fail the entire term." Her brown eyes pleaded with Andi. "You won't carry tales to her, will you? I'm sorry. When somethin' spooks me, the words just fly out—whether I want 'em to or not. I try and try, but talking like a lady is hard work, 'specially where I come from."

Andi didn't know what to say. She crossed the room and sat down on her bed. Then she cast a sideways glance at the stranger. Andi wanted to laugh. The girl looked so funny, with her hair all a tangle and her eyes as large and round as an owl's. But it wouldn't be polite to laugh, so she said, "No, I won't tell."

The girl let out a long, heartfelt sigh and returned to her bed. She plopped down and picked up her needlework. "It's these blamed . . . uh . . . I mean these *horrible* dresser scarves that have my belly tied in knots. As much as my mama would like, I fear I won't ever turn out a decent piece of needlework. This teeny needle and my clumsy fingers can't seem to work out an agreement. I've been here since last fall and this is all I've managed to finish." She held it up for Andi's inspection. "By the way, my name's Jenny Grant."

"I'm Andi." She took the wrinkled needlework and bit her lip. *Oh, my! Even I embroider better than this, and that's not saying much.* "Well, it does need a little work," she said, passing it back. "But Miss Whitaker can't expect more from you than your best."

"Maybe not. But the highfalutin' young ladies here sure expect plenty." She crossed her arms over her chest. "It's not my fault I was brought up in the backwoods rather than in the city. It's not my fault I've got a passel of logger brothers to run with, rather than a sister. Mama tried to make me a lady, but it didn't work out so good."

Andi shoved herself against the wall, pulled her knees up under her skirt and asked, "How did you end up here?"

Jenny stretched out on her bed. She clasped her hands behind her head and stared up at the chandelier hanging from the ceiling. "A friend wrote Mama and told her about this girls' school in San Francisco—only a couple of weeks away by clipper ship—where I'd learn all I needed to turn out a 'finished' lady. So she talked Papa into sending me here for one year." She turned and looked at Andi. "Oh, how my brothers laughed when they heard that! 'No fancy school can turn *you* into a lady, Jenny,' my brother Eli said." She sat up and clenched her fists. "But I'll show Eli. I'll show them all that I can be a lady. The finest lady in Washington Territory." She sighed. "I try so hard, but the other girls turn their noses up at me. I haven't made any friends here, unless"—she gave Andi a crooked smile—"unless you call occasionally smiling at the little China girl down in the kitchen making friends. She's probably the only person around here worse off than me."

Andi, who was resting her chin on her knees, sat up straight. "You know Lin Mei?"

Jenny shrugged. "Not really. Like I said, I smile at her sometimes when she brings me fresh linens. We've exchanged a couple of words, but she spooks real easy. Like a rabbit watching out for a hungry hawk."

Andi nodded. Lin Mei was definitely a scared rabbit. "Maybe we

can help her. I met her this morning, and I feel real sorry for her."
For the first time since reluctantly agreeing to go to Aunt Rebecca's,
Andi felt a glimmer of hope. Jenny was different from the image
Andi harbored of a typical, nose-in-the-air young lady boarding at an
elegant finishing school. Fresh from the backwoods and stuck in the
same situation as she, Jenny was a welcome breeze from the Pacific
Ocean—invigorating, if perhaps a bit salty in her speech.

"Enough about me," Jenny was saying. "We've got a few minutes
until the supper bell rings. Tell me your story."

Andi grinned. She knew that tonight, when she curled up under
her quilt in this unfamiliar place, she would remember to thank God
for sending a wild, red-haired girl to be her friend.

*Chapter Seven*

# A RIDE IN THE PARK

D ear Mother . . ." Andi gripped her pen and scratched the greeting onto a sheet of academy stationery. "I am settling in at school and doing well in my studies." It wasn't *exactly* a lie. She was doing well in Latin and mathematics. Composition was satisfactory, and she was caught up in history—thanks to Mr. Foster insisting last fall that she memorize dozens of important dates in America's colonization. However, French was definitely a problem, and she preferred not to worry her mother with a bad report of music and drawing.

She dipped her pen in the ink well and continued her letter. "It turns out that I am boarding at Miss Whitaker's. I was angry with Aunt Rebecca about that until I met my roommate. Her name is Jenny, and she's from Tacoma, in Washington Territory. I looked on a map, and Tacoma is truly in the middle of nowhere. Her father owns a sawmill, which has done well the last twenty years. Jenny has four older brothers and one younger one. They cut down the trees, saw them up, and ship the lumber to California to shore up the mines."

Andi stopped and scratched at an itchy spot on her leg. She didn't think she'd ever get used to wearing the woolen stockings that were part of the school's uniform. One week had passed, and she was tired of wearing the same thing—day in and day out—except on Sundays, when the girls dressed in their best and attended church.

"This afternoon we're taking the cable car to Golden Gate Park. The school boards a number of horses at the park, and I earned the privilege of going along this Sunday." She didn't add that riding in the park couldn't take the place of riding Taffy. She'd made up her mind that she would not complain in her letters home, at least not much; she would keep a stiff upper lip, study her lessons, and mark off the days until Justin returned to take her home.

"I saw Kate and the kids yesterday, but did not stay overnight. Thomas brought me back to school after supper. I have no idea how he finds his way around this city, especially in the dark. There aren't nearly enough street lamps to suit me, and it's a long way from Aunt Rebecca's to the school.

"I haven't visited the seashore yet, and I don't care to. The ocean seems to seep into the very air, and I always feel chilled.

"I miss you all. Give everyone my love. Tell Rosa she can ride Taffy if she wants to. If school opens early, please come for me."

With a flourish of her pen, Andi finished her one-page letter. "Your loving (but lonely) daughter, Andi." Then she thought of something. "P.S.," she wrote, "The cable cars are the best part of San Francisco. I have ridden in them twice. So far they appear safe, but it's a long, long way down the hill. I have decided that if something breaks, I will jump off really quick."

Andi blotted her letter, carefully cleaned her pen tip, and found an envelope just as the jingling of a bell sounded from downstairs. Time to go! She could barely contain her eagerness to get back on a horse—even if the horse was not Taffy.

Half an hour later, crammed into the cable car with twenty young ladies and Miss Whitaker, Andi wondered if this outing would be worth the trouble. Her riding habit—a ridiculous combination of a heavy, dark-blue woolen skirt and tightly fitted jacket—squeezed her until she could scarcely breathe. The sun had burned away what remained of the morning fog, and it shone down bright and warm. Andi wished she could trade the silly little silk hat she was wearing for her practical, wide-brimmed felt hat back home.

"I'm going to roast in this get-up," she whispered to Jenny, who sat beside her. She shoved her thick, dark hair away from her face. *If only I could braid it!* But no, young ladies at Miss Whitaker's did not wear their hair in two sloppy braids.

With a jerk and a clang, the cable car came to a stop at the end of the line, Golden Gate Park. Andi forgot her discomfort and followed the others to the stables, where a number of horses waited, saddled and bridled, for their eager riders.

Andi was shown her mount for the afternoon, a quiet, patient-looking gray gelding with half-closed eyes and a drooping head. "Howdy, fella," she greeted him. She stroked his nose, slapped his shoulder, and circled him. "I hope you don't fall asleep on me," she whispered in his ear. Then she turned to the stable hand, who was holding tightly to the horse's bridle. "What's his name?"

"Tornado," the boy replied with an impish grin. "But we call him *El Perezoso*—the Lazy One."

Andi sighed, resigned. She grasped the reins and found the stirrup. Then she frowned. "What's wrong with this saddle?"

"Nothing's wrong with the saddle, miss," the boy assured her. "I checked it myself only moments ago. Don't be afraid."

Andi yanked at the long folds of her riding skirt and glared at the boy. "I'm not afraid."

"Andrea," Miss Whitaker called from a carriage that pulled up beside her. "We're ready to go. Please mount up and join us, if you would."

Andi looked up. The other girls, including Jenny, were seated on their horses. In a flash, Andi knew what was wrong with her saddle. She felt her face grow hot. Here she was, the best young rider in Fresno County and the winner of the Fourth of July race last summer, and she didn't know how to ride sidesaddle. Nor did she want to learn.

She made no move to mount.

"I assumed you can ride," Miss Whitaker said. "Was I mistaken?"

Andi shook her head. "No, ma'am, I can ride. But I . . . I . . . ride astride." She heard gasps from the other students, along with three or four snickers.

"I see," Miss Whitaker said quietly. "Well, do the best you can today. Tomorrow Mr. Hunter can arrange *proper* riding lessons for you back at the school."

More snickers.

Andi's face flamed. *Riding lessons!*

"Help the young lady mount," Miss Whitaker ordered the stable boy. He jumped to obey.

Shaking, and with her heart thumping in humiliation, Andi allowed the boy to help her up. For the first time in her life, she felt a twinge of fear on the back of a horse. Tornado must have felt it too. He laid his ears back and shook his mane.

"Easy, boy." Andi hooked her right leg around the pommel and smoothed down her skirt. "I'm sure I can figure this out. Just give me a minute." But as she fell in behind the other young ladies and Miss Whitaker's carriage, she knew it would take more than a minute to figure out this new, and totally absurd, way of riding.

The hour dragged by. Andi wished with all her might that she were back on the Circle C, she and Taffy flying over the rangeland instead of *El Perezoso* clomping along slower than Andi could walk. She yawned and gave Jenny a bored look. "And to think I worked extra hard all week to earn this . . . *privilege.*"

Jenny laughed.

Andi paid little attention to her horse and even less to keeping her seat, until it was too late. As the parade of students rounded the curve that wound its way back to the stables, Tornado's head snapped up. His ears pricked forward. In an unexpected burst of speed, he began to hightail it back to the barn. Caught off guard by her own carelessness, hampered by the awkward saddle, and fearing for her life, Andi held on with grim determination. *No horse will ever dump me*, she promised herself.

But that's exactly what Tornado did. The horse came to a skidding stop next to the stables, and Andi tumbled to the ground in an unladylike heap. She lay there, stunned and aching, and tried to catch her breath.

"Oh, Andi! Are you all right?" Jenny's voice seemed to come from far away.

Andi bit back a groan, looked up, and found herself surrounded by astonished young ladies and stable hands. Florence Burnside, the oldest of the students, expressed aloud what Andi knew the others were thinking:

"Is that a special kind of trick-riding you do on your ranch? Looks dangerous to me." Then she and the rest of the girls dissolved in laughter before Miss Whitaker drew up and shooed them back to the stables.

"Merciful heavens, child!" Miss Whitaker stepped down from the carriage and hurried to Andi's side. "You could have been killed. I've heard more than one tale of ladies' skirts becoming entangled in the saddle, and the victim dragged alongside the horse." She helped Andi to her feet and declared, "Most certainly you will begin lessons tomorrow."

Once back in her room, Andi peeled off her riding clothes, threw herself face down on her bed, and moaned. She hurt all over, inside and out.

Jenny snorted. "Oh, I *am* sorry!" she apologized between giggles. "I don't mean to laugh. But the look on your face when Tornado dumped you was worth the whole dull afternoon."

Andi groaned at the memory. Her longed-for horseback ride in Golden Gate Park had begun and ended in shambles, and it was her own fault.

She felt a gentle hand rub her back and rolled over. Jenny was looking down at her, the smile wiped from her face. "Pay no mind to the others. Everybody here knows who your Aunt Rebecca is and how she supports this school. They all know your family is one of the richest in the state. They teased you 'cause they know it's the only chance they'll ever get. In everything else, you can hold your own—ladylike—with any of 'em. You might not like acting like a lady, but at least you know how, when you've a mind to. Not like me. I nearly keel over every time I curtsy, and I walk like a logger. I'll never fit in, no matter how much money my papa has."

Andi sat up and gave her friend a hug. "Thanks, Jenny. You know what? Now that it's over, I reckon it *was* kind of funny. And no less than I deserve. I broke the most important rule of our ranch—never, *never* let your guard down around a horse. That's how my father died. He was thrown from his horse during a roundup." She sighed. "So . . . you can laugh as much as you want. But"—she pulled away from Jenny and waggled a finger in her face—"don't you ever tell my brothers I got dumped."

Jenny swiped a finger across her camisole in a huge X. "Cross my heart and hope to die," she chanted with a giggle. "Don't I know what brothers are like!"

They were still laughing when Andi heard a quiet scratching at the door.

"I wonder who's here," Andi said. It was late Sunday afternoon and nearly time for supper. She pulled on a pale yellow housecoat, tossed her unruly tangle of long, dark curls behind her shoulder, and opened the door a crack.

"Linens," Lin Mei whispered.

Andi smiled and threw open the door. "Come on in."

Lin Mei shook her head. "Please to take these," she urged, shoving an armful of clean towels and sheets toward Andi. She looked ready to flee.

Andi took the linens and quickly passed them to Jenny, who was standing behind her. "Why can't you come in and visit a bit? We won't tell Miss Whitaker."

Lin Mei clasped her hands and began to wring them. "Feng Chee . . . he . . . he say you bad. You *fahn quai*—white devils. Must stay away. *Fahn quai* lock Lin Mei up. Sell Lin Mei far away. *Fahn quai* full of evil spirits." She bowed and stepped back. "I go now."

Andi followed Lin Mei into the hallway. "Surely you don't believe all that. Has anyone here ever tried to do these terrible things to you?"

Lin Mei shook her head. "Feng Chee tell stories of girls falling into hands of white devils. You and girl with fire hair talk to Lin Mei. Feng Chee very angry. He say you"—she pointed at Andi—"very bad. Make much talk. Much trouble." Tears welled up in her eyes. "Must go. Much work."

Jenny poked her head through the doorway. "It's Sunday. Don't you ever get a chance to rest, or to run and play?"

Lin Mei wrinkled her brow. "No run and play. No rest. Must go now. Much washing. Much sewing in Chinatown. Come back when sun up."

Andi's heart went out to the little Chinese girl. No play. No rest. Nothing but work, work, work, and no doubt always dodging Feng Chee's or Wen Shu's quick tempers and cruel beatings. To top it off, the cook had fed Lin Mei terrible lies about Andi just because she'd talked to her. *That Feng Chee fellow is meaner than a rattlesnake*, she decided with a scowl.

She wanted to do something kind for Lin Mei, something to show her that Americans were not white devils, or at least most of them weren't. What would make Lin Mei smile? *What makes Betsy smile?* She snapped her fingers. "I've got it! Stay right here," she told her.

Lin Mei watched with solemn eyes as Andi brushed past Jenny and disappeared into her room. A minute later she returned, twirling a length of string. "I can play a game with this string. Would you like me to show you?"

Lin Mei shook her head. "Must . . . go." But she didn't move. She stared at the string, bit her lip, then gave a tiny nod. It was clear that her curiosity had been stirred by the word *game.*

Andi sat down in her housecoat in the middle of the hallway and began to twist the string around her fingers. "My niece Betsy loves this game. It's called Cat's Cradle." In no time, Andi had Lin Mei holding out eager fingers to try the next pattern in the string game.

For a moment, a bright spark replaced the dull, sad look in her eyes. *This girl is smart as a whip*, Andi thought. She wondered what else might be locked up in the Chinese girl's mind, crushed by the despair of her servitude.

Then came the miracle. After an especially difficult twist, when the string turned into a hopeless tangle on Andi's fingers, Lin Mei giggled.

Jenny and Andi exchanged pleased smiles over the child's head.

"If you want, we can play this game every time you bring us our linens," Andi said. She untangled the string and dropped it into Lin Mei's tiny, rough palm.

Before Lin Mei could answer, a loud, stunned voice rang through the hallway. "What are you doing on the floor in your housecoats, playing with the servants?"

Andi, Jenny, and Lin Mei sprang to their feet.

Florence and her best friend, Lydia Sharp, stood staring at them in shock. "I can understand Jennifer Grant's ignorance," Lydia said, "but you, Andrea Carter, should know better. Wait until Miss Whitaker hears about this."

Andi bristled. "You don't have to go bleating to Miss Whitaker. We weren't doing any harm."

"So you say," Florence put in. "But I'm afraid Miss Whitaker must be the judge of that."

"Please, Florence," Andi pleaded with the older girl, "let it go. This once." She wasn't worried about facing the headmistress and being punished. Her only concern was what would happen to Lin Mei.

Florence didn't answer. She and Lydia turned their backs on the younger girls and disappeared inside their room next door.

Jenny clenched her fists. "If those two give us trouble, I'll knock 'em clear into next Tuesday."

"No you won't," Andi said wearily. "You're learning to be a lady, remember?" Then she looked at the Chinese girl, standing frozen beside her. "I hope we can still be friends, Lin Mei."

But Lin Mei was shaking her head. "No . . . no . . . not good. Feng Chee very angry. I am *mui tsai* . . . slave. No time for *fahn quai* friends." With a half-sob, she dashed away.

## Chapter Eight

# ANDI MAKES A PROMISE

True to their threat, Florence and Lydia informed the headmistress of what they had witnessed. Early Monday morning, Andi again found herself summoned to Miss Whitaker's office, only this time she wasn't alone. Jenny stood beside her, which was a small comfort. She listened to the headmistress's pronouncement of judgment with half an ear. All her thoughts focused on what fate awaited Lin Mei.

"Your riding privileges in the park are withdrawn for the next two Sundays," Miss Whitaker said. She turned her dark gaze on Andi. "As well as visits to your aunt for those Saturdays, Andrea. When Rebecca learns why, I'm sure she'll be as grieved over this as I am and will support my decision."

"Yes, ma'am." Andi knew Aunt Rebecca would certainly not approve of her niece hobnobbing with the servants, no matter what the reason. Especially when she'd been warned to stay away from them. *Why is it so wrong to be friendly with Lin Mei? What could it possibly hurt?*

"Andrea, did you hear me?"

Miss Whitaker's question cut into Andi's musing like a splash of cold water against her face. She jerked her head up. "I'm sorry. No, I didn't hear you."

"I was saying that along with your privileges being withdrawn, you girls receive two disgrace marks, which will be entered into your records."

This came as no surprise. "Yes, ma'am." She cast a sidelong glance at Jenny, who rolled her eyes while Miss Whitaker shuffled her papers and reached for her pen and ink. *Ask her*, her friend mouthed silently and gave her a nudge.

"What about Lin Mei?" Andi blurted before she changed her mind. "It wasn't her fault. You can't blame her. She didn't want to stay, but I kept her there. Please, Miss Whitaker, what will happen to her?"

Miss Whitaker's eyes opened wide at Andi's pleading. "There's no need to get so distressed over a servant. I spoke with Feng Chee, and he assures me the child's indiscretion will be dealt with quickly and suitably."

Andi cringed at what this most likely meant. Lin Mei would suffer for not heeding her master's warning, and it was Andi's fault. Her heart ached for the little girl, and there wasn't a thing she could do about it. Oh, how she wished she were a grownup, and a man besides! She'd light into Feng Chee and give him a taste of his own medicine.

"Can't you talk to Feng Chee and tell him it wasn't . . . ?" Andi stopped talking at the look of finality on Miss Whitaker's face.

"The matter is settled, Andrea." She checked her timepiece and rose from the chair, indicating the meeting was over. "You should have thought about what might happen to the child before you disregarded my instructions. Now, girls, to your classes. Quickly. You do not want to be marked tardy."

"Yes, ma'am."

Andi looked at Jenny, who was clenching her fists, clearly trying to keep hold of her temper. Andi felt the same way, but she knew it would do no good to antagonize Miss Whitaker further. Arguing would only result in more disgrace marks, and Andi couldn't afford any more of those. So she turned to go.

Jenny stiffly followed Andi's lead, and together they hastened from Miss Whitaker's office.

There was no time to chat as they hurried down the hallway toward the mathematics class they shared. Andi could tell that Jenny was fit to be tied over what had happened yesterday and during the short meeting with Miss Whitaker this morning. She'd known her friend only one short week, but in that time she'd learned a number of things. It was quite possible that Jenny Grant was even more reckless and impulsive than Andi. She could see it in her friend's flushed cheeks and tight jaw, and in the way she stomped down the hallway a dozen steps ahead of her. *She does walk like a logger*, Andi observed with a quiet chuckle.

"Jenny!" She caught up to her friend outside the classroom door. "Don't go off half-cocked. You told me you want to be a lady. A lady controls herself and accepts what she can't change." *I can't believe I'm saying this. I sound just like Mother.* She laid a calming hand on Jenny's arm. "Instead of flying down to the kitchen and giving Feng Chee a piece of your mind, let's think of a way to *really* help Lin Mei."

Jenny's eyes lit up. "How?"

Andi grinned. "My riding lessons start this afternoon. I bet Juan Carlos knows plenty about this city and its people. Perhaps he can help us."

"The stable boy?" Jenny looked skeptical.

Andi placed her hand on the doorknob of their classroom. "It's worth a try." Then she opened the door, and the two girls slipped into their seats just before the clock struck nine.

Andi was pleased that Miss Whitaker had not taken away her riding lessons. Although she had no desire to "correct any poor horsemanship habits picked up on the ranch," as Aunt Rebecca had told her several days ago, the chance to spend time with the horses had fallen nicely into her lap. Her humiliation from yesterday had turned into an unexpected blessing, and she wasn't about to let any silly pride get in her way.

"The others can tease me for not riding like a lady," she said as she made her way to the stables. "I don't care. I get a free hour every day to talk to Juan Carlos. This could not have worked out better if I'd planned it myself."

There was only one snag: It was not Juan Carlos waiting for her in the stable.

"You don't look pleased to see me," Mr. Hunter rasped, giving her a leer. His bushy eyebrows locked over his forehead in a thick, gray line. "Well, the feeling's mutual. I got better things to do than waste my time mollycoddling a spoiled schoolgirl who can't keep her seat on a horse." Andi's stomach lurched. Mr. Hunter's words felt like a slap to her face. Was he refusing to let her ride? "I-I don't understand," she managed to say.

Mr. Hunter grunted and spat a stream of tobacco juice that fell just shy of Andi's feet. "The young ladies all had their instruction last fall with the riding master, Mister Tate—the dandy from up the hill." He motioned toward Nob Hill. "Now the missus says I gotta teach *you*." He leaned forward, shook a gnarled finger at her, and barked, "That ain't part of my job. The missus and me have an understanding. I take care of the grounds. I hitch up the carriage. If a scholar wants to ride, I see to the horses. Other than that, we keep out of each other's way."

*I can see why,* Andi wanted to snap back, but she held her tongue. No wonder Juan Carlos feared this man. Mr. Hunter was callous, rude, and offensive. Even the greenest of her brothers' ranch hands had better manners than this oaf. Andi didn't understand why Miss Whitaker allowed him anywhere near her fancy school or her pupils. *Maybe he's good at his job,* she thought. The grounds certainly looked well kept, and the school's horses cared for. *Maybe Miss Whitaker's afraid of him.*

Whatever the reason, she wasn't going to let him keep her from riding today. If Mr. Hunter thought she was going to burst into tears and run away at his rude manner, he was greatly mistaken. She pushed aside her own uneasiness, drew herself up, and looked the cranky old man in the eye. "If you don't want to teach me, then perhaps your stable hand could."

Mr. Hunter's eyebrows shot up. "The Mex? He's good for nothing but mucking out stalls and digging in the dirt."

"Miss Whitaker seemed insistent about the riding lessons. Shall I tell her that you refuse to follow her wishes?" Andi turned to go.

"Hold on, miss," Mr. Hunter relented. He seemed taken back at Andi's words. When she faced him, he thrust the reins into her hands. "I'll send the Mex over. Just don't be bothering me again, you hear?"

It was settled. Each day when Andi appeared at the stable for her lesson, Juan Carlos greeted her with a sunny smile and a polite bow. She quickly discovered that he was an excellent horseman and a patient teacher. When she complained about having to learn to ride sidesaddle, Juan Carlos scolded her like an older brother:

"You are foolish to hold on to such a childish notion. As you learned the hard way, knowing only one riding style can put you at a disadvantage. You would be wise to learn all you can."

When he put it that way, Andi was forced to agree, and she set her mind to conquering her prejudice against the awkward saddle. It didn't take long.

"I don't know how many days Miss Whitaker will let me go on taking lessons," she confided to Juan Carlos two weeks later. As usual, she waited to talk with the "lowly stable hand" until they were out of reach of Mr. Hunter's exceptional hearing. The old man prowled the grounds of the academy; one never knew where he might pop up.

As soon as Juan Carlos led Andi's horse along the trail near the perimeter of the school, they fell into the relaxed, easy friendship that had blossomed between them. "The truth is," Juan Carlos remarked as he yanked on Big Red's lead line, "you needed no lessons after the second day." He grinned up at her. "I'm surprised the *señora* has allowed you to continue this long." Two weeks of lessons and conversations with Juan Carlos had gone by quickly.

Andi settled herself more comfortably on the large horse. "If you'd seen me that Sunday, you'd probably think I needed a month of lessons. It was humiliating." She returned his grin. "But I'm glad it happened. How else could I have wrangled this much time with the horses and learned about you and your family, besides? And you seem to know everything about San Francisco."

Juan Carlos agreed. "*Sí*. I know the city well. I have lived here since I was a child." He turned and walked backward as he led the horse. "Someday I must show you the sand dunes and the beach." He sighed. "*Ay, señorita*, you have not lived until you have raced a fast horse along the shore."

"Perhaps when my brother comes for me, we can take a day and race there with"—she grimaced at the seat that chafed her—"proper saddles or none at all."

"It would be my pleasure," Juan said.

Andi glanced ahead. The trail would soon circle back to the stables, and her lesson would come to an end. For two weeks she had skirted the subject of helping Lin Mei, much to Jenny's dismay. Jenny wanted action. Now. Instead, Andi had encouraged Juan Carlos to tell her about interesting sights to see in San Francisco. Unfortunately, Chinatown was not on his list of places to visit. The time had come to ask him outright. "Do you know anything about Chinatown?"

Juan stopped short and brought Big Red to a halt. He gave Andi a puzzled look and nodded. "I am no stranger to Chinatown. It is an odd, foreign place. Why do you wish to know?"

"For one thing, it's only a few blocks from here. It might be fun to go down and see what it's like."

Juan Carlos's expression turned thoughtful. "To be sure, many people visit Chinatown. There are lanterns and flowers; herb and incense shops; restaurants, groceries, and laundries. Many visit the Chinese theater. Everywhere there are vendors selling foods of all kinds. The streets overflow with people dressed in strange clothes who speak a language you cannot understand." He paused. "Most of Chinatown is home to respectable, hard-working families, but there is a dark, evil side. I advise you to leave Chinatown to the Chinese."

A slight breeze rustled the shrubbery. Big Red stamped an impatient hoof. It was getting late. "Is it true, Juan Carlos," Andi asked softly, "that there are slaves in Chinatown?"

Juan yanked on the horse's lead rope and started down the trail, heading home. "*Sí*. You will always find wicked, lawless people in any society. It is no different here. There are some Chinese who buy or kidnap young girls from their own country and smuggle them into the United States. For a small bribe to crooked, white immigration officials, they can even get false papers." He shook his head sadly. "Chinatown swallows up these little ones and spits them out as servants, with no hope of escape."

Andi's blood burned hot as she listened to Juan Carlos's bleak words. The fact that Chinatown carried out a thriving slave trade was clearly no secret. Even a lowly stable hand knew what went on only a few short blocks from Miss Whitaker's Academy. "Why don't the rich folks up on Nob Hill do something about it?"

Juan brought Big Red to a stop. "That is a question I cannot answer." He caught her gaze and said, "Now it is my turn to ask the questions."

"All right," Andi said. She'd learned more than she wanted to know, and it had confirmed her worst fears: Lin Mei was without a doubt one of those poor girls trapped in slavery. "I'll answer your questions, but you can't tell anybody."

"*¡Señorita!*" Juan raised his hands and smiled. "Who would I tell? Who at the school speaks my language but you?"

Andi relaxed. "I don't want Miss Whitaker finding out that I'm not letting a certain matter go, like she told me to."

"Agreed." He reached out and rubbed Big Red's nose. "I want to know why you are asking questions about Chinatown and slavery. This is a subject not fitting for a well-bred, proper young lady."

"Jenny and I want to help Lin Mei get away from Feng Chee," Andi blurted, "and we thought you might know how we could do it."

Juan Carlos stiffened. He dropped the lead rope and rounded on her. "Are you *loco*? She is the cook's niece."

"So everybody says. But Lin Mei says different. She told me she came over on a boat from Canton and was sold to Feng Chee and Wen Shu. After listening to you, I believe it. She's scared to death of them, and no wonder! Have you seen how they treat her?"

"I have seen," Juan Carlos said. His dark eyes smoldered. "But there is nothing you can do about it. You cannot change what goes on in Chinatown, nor should you meddle in its affairs. It is a dangerous place, full of secrets. There are hundreds of girls in the same position as your little friend. You cannot rescue them all."

"I don't want to rescue them all. Only Lin Mei." She gave Juan Carlos an imploring look. "Will you help me?"

Juan Carlos let out a long, slow breath. Then he reached out and grasped the lead rope. Without a word, he set out at a brisk walk. Big Red broke into a trot.

"Juan Carlos," Andi called after him, "will you help me?"

The young man stopped. The horse stopped. Juan Carlos turned and regarded Andi sorrowfully. Then he shook his head. "No, *señorita*, I will not help you. I *cannot* help you. This job is my livelihood. If *Señor* Hunter or *Señora* Whitaker learned I was involved in such a *loco* scheme as spiriting away a young Chinese girl from her rightful family, I could lose my position. I could be arrested for kidnapping."

"But—"

"*¡Basta ya!* Enough!" Juan Carlos shouted, slicing the air with his hand. Then he seemed to regret his outburst. "I know you mean well, and your heart is tender toward this poor, unfortunate child. But here is the truth of the matter: Lin Mei is better off where she is, even if she is a slave. She could be in a far worse situation. If you meddle in this business, you could cause more trouble for the girl. Bad trouble."

Andi opened her mouth to protest, but Juan Carlos cut her off.

"I see you do not believe me, but I know what I'm talking about. I too am a servant. Perhaps not a slave, but I might as well be," he said bitterly. "It is sometimes better to leave things as they are. Otherwise you may bring down the wrath of not only your headmistress, but also of Feng Chee. He is a dangerous man—more dangerous than any cook should be. I would not want this *hombre* angry with *me*."

Andi dropped her head and stared at her lap. Suddenly, she felt Juan's cold fingers curl around her hand and grip it tightly. She looked at him in surprise.

"Promise me, *señorita*, that you will do as the *señora* instructs and let this matter go. You will not steal Lin Mei away from her . . . family."

He held Andi's gaze and waited for an answer. *He knows!* Her heart skipped a beat. *He knows Lin Mei is a slave, and he's afraid I might do something reckless. He's worried about me.* For an instant she imagined herself back on the ranch, and Chad had yanked her out of yet another risky situation. *Promise me, Andi!* Juan Carlos sounded just like her brother.

She swallowed. "All right. I'll let it go. I'll pray, instead. I'll ask God to make Feng Chee and Wen Shu treat Lin Mei kinder, and that Lin Mei will be strong."

Juan Carlos nodded. He released her hand and smiled at her. "*Sí, señorita*. God can look after the little girl much better than you can." He seemed relieved. "And now, we must return before *Señor* Hunter comes looking for us."

With a tug on the lead rope, he raced down the trail.

## Chapter Nine

# MISSING!

It was a difficult promise to keep.

"You promised *what?*" Jenny leaped from her bed, eyes flashing, and stomped across their small room. Hands on her hips, she let Andi know what she thought. "I've watched since last fall as that China girl flitted from one miserable task to another around here. Nobody in the entire school seems to care about her. They hardly know she exists. All Florence or Lydia or Madeline notice is whether Lin Mei delivers their linens on time or if their shoes are properly polished. I've tried since I got here to make friends with her, but I couldn't get her to say more than two words to me."

Jenny threw herself down on her bed and glared at Andi. "Then you came. I don't know how you did it, but you talked to Lin Mei your first day here. You taught her a game. She *laughed.* And now you say you're going to let it go?" Jenny shook her head. "I don't understand. What did that stable boy tell you, anyway?"

"Enough to know that by trying to help Lin Mei, we could make things worse for her."

"What could be worse than being screamed at, knocked around, and worked half to death?" Jenny demanded in a huff. She flung her wild snarl of red hair behind her shoulder, snatched up a brush from the washstand, and began vigorously attacking the tangles.

Andi's stomach twisted at Jenny's words. This was their first quarrel since becoming friends. *I've never had a girlfriend like this before. Jenny's nothing like Rosa.* Andi considered Rosa Garduño her best friend, but she knew Rosa couldn't forget the fact that she was the Carters' hired servant. Rosa might disagree with Andi, but she never stood up to her. Andi's good friend, Cory Blake, stood up to her, and they argued constantly, but . . .

*I don't want to quarrel with Jenny. She's right, but there's nothing we can do.* "Well, then," she said aloud, "what's your bright idea? Not that I'd go along with it," she hastily added, "but tell me."

Jenny yanked at her tangled curls, trying to make them lie flat. Then she snatched up a ribbon and tied the whole mess away from her face. "I don't have any ideas," she confessed with a shrug. "I reckon that's why I got so riled at you—because I was mostly riled at myself and at that ol' 'fraidy cat, the stable boy."

"His name is Juan Carlos," Andi corrected her friend. She looked at the clock. It was nearly suppertime. With a heavy heart, she began to pull off her riding habit and make herself presentable for the evening meal. But she wasn't hungry. How could she sit at the table and pretend everything was all right when she knew that—hidden away in the kitchen—little Lin Mei was struggling simply to make it through another day?

Yet she had to let it go. She'd promised.

"Well, whatever his name is," Jenny said, "surely he could have given you one teeny weeny idea."

"Like what?" Andi yanked a pale yellow and green dress from her wardrobe. "Burst into the kitchen, snatch Lin Mei out from under Feng Chee's nose, and start running through the streets? Where would we go? What would we do with her? Juan Carlos told me I was *loco* to even think about trying to get Lin Mei away from Feng Chee."

Jenny brightened. "Perhaps he talked so fast you didn't catch his Spanish. I miss plenty of words in French class. Maybe you misunderstood him?"

Andi shook her head. "No, Jenny. I speak Spanish as well as I speak English. There was no misunderstanding." She struggled to pull the frock over her head. When she could speak again, her words were final. "The matter is settled. We'd best do what Miss Whitaker says." She tied back her own dark waves with a wide ribbon and slammed her wardrobe door shut just as the dinner bell tinkled its warning from outside their door.

"I ain't hungry," Jenny pouted. She was clearly in no mood to refine her speech.

"I'm not either," Andi said, "but gathering for meals is expected. Do you really want to find yourself in Miss Whitaker's office this evening? I don't."

Without waiting for Jenny, she left the room and headed downstairs for supper.

Their disagreement didn't go away. For the next week, Jenny spouted ideas on how to help Lin Mei. Andi stood firm in her promise to Juan Carlos to let the matter go, but she worried about the Chinese girl. She hadn't seen her all week. No doubt nasty old Feng Chee was keeping her far, far away from the "white devils."

By the time Latin class rolled around each afternoon, Andi was exhausted from trying to stay on her mental carousel. Today was no different. She was smothering a yawn when Miss Tatum, the Latin instructor, rapped her ruler sharply against her desk. "Your attention please, scholars. Our headmistress has an announcement."

Andi pulled her sleepy gaze from the page of unending Latin verbs and looked up. She blinked in surprise to see Miss Whitaker standing next to Miss Tatum at the front of the room. *I didn't even hear her come in. I must be tired.* Nothing was more tedious than memorizing Latin verbs, so Andi welcomed any interruption during this last class of the day. Miss Whitaker's unexpected entrance should have captured her attention.

Andi perked up at once. She glanced at the clock: a quarter before the hour. If Miss Whitaker talked long enough, school would be over for the day. No more Latin!

Miss Whitaker had very little to say, but at her first words, Andi's mouth dropped open.

"I am dismissing class early so you may assemble in the common room with the rest of the scholars to hear what I have to say. It is a matter of grave importance that affects our school." She nodded at the teacher, turned, and abruptly left the room.

Miss Tatum picked up her bell and gave it a few quick shakes.

Andi closed her Latin book, gathered up the rest of her materials, and waited for the ten other girls to make ready to leave. When Miss Tatum nodded, the pupils rose from their seats and filed out of the classroom in a neat, silent line.

A few minutes later, as they assembled in the large room reserved for special school gatherings, Andi felt a squeeze on her elbow. Jenny edged alongside Andi and whispered, "I wonder what all the ruckus is about."

Andi grinned. "Who cares? Class ended early, and that's cause for celebration, whatever the reason."

Miss Whitaker walked to the front of the assembled students and motioned for silence. "Young ladies, please. Your attention."

There were no chairs. The twenty students stood in rows, their attention fixed on the headmistress. Andi had to stand on tiptoes to see over the girls in front of her. She clutched her schoolbooks in one hand and reached out with the other to steady herself against Jenny.

"I have disturbing news. The kitchen servant, Lin Mei, is missing."

Andi gasped and tightened her grip on Jenny's arm.

The other girls remained silent. They seemed confused, clearly wondering why Miss Whitaker would assemble the entire school together to tell them about a missing servant girl. What did it matter? Florence shrugged and shifted her books to her other arm.

Miss Whitaker stood ramrod straight and clutched a handkerchief in her hands as she waited for her words to sink in. Clearly, she was troubled. "Our school's cook, Feng Chee, is beside himself with worry. He and Wen Shu have looked everywhere, but the child has vanished." Her expression turned hard. "Feng Chee believes Lin Mei became frightened after listening to foolish tales from some of you. I assured him this is not true. None of my young ladies would do such a thing." She sighed. "But he is convinced of it. Why else would the child run away from the 'white devils,' as they call us?"

*The only tales Lin Mei hears come from Feng Chee*, Andi thought with scorn. *If she's really gone, I hope she's run far, far away.*

"Miss Whitaker?" From Andi's left, Lydia Sharp raised a hand.

"Yes, Lydia?"

"I've never associated with the China girl or spoken to her. I don't think any of us have, except . . ." She paused and turned her gaze on Andi and Jenny. She didn't finish her sentence.

Andi felt Jenny rustle beside her. Andi gave her friend a pinch on the arm to silence her.

Miss Whitaker nodded. "I realize that, Lydia. Unfortunately, there is more to this incident. A number of small but valuable items have been stolen—a brooch, a pair of earrings, a bracelet. They are heirlooms from my grandmother. I kept them secured in a small, locked case in my office. The case is missing."

The room exploded in groans, gasps, and murmurs of outrage. "The China girl stole them," Andi heard someone whisper behind her.

"Are our things safe?" Florence asked over the clamor.

"Ladies, ladies," Miss Whitaker scolded, "your voices, please. Yes, Florence, I believe your personal articles are safe. But it might be wise to go through your rooms and make sure nothing is missing." She shook her head. "Never in all my years as headmistress has a scandal like this taken place."

"How do you know Lin Mei took the jewelry?" Andi asked in a loud, clear voice.

Lydia whirled on her. "Isn't it obvious? Lin Mei is missing. Miss Whitaker's jewelry is missing. It makes perfect sense to me."

"I agree," Miss Whitaker said. "This is why I've assembled you here. It's possible that Lin Mei is nearby. A small child wouldn't wander alone in the city. Perhaps she's curled up in a corner somewhere, hiding. A thorough search of the school and the grounds will show Feng Chee that we are concerned enough to help him recover his niece"—she paused—"and my precious heirlooms. We must find her."

*Sure*, Andi thought, *find the little girl, find the jewels*. Miss Whitaker seemed more concerned over her missing jewelry than with the fact that Lin Mei might be in danger.

"Miss Whitaker," she asked, "what happens when you find her?"

Miss Whitaker shook her head sadly. "I'm afraid I must have servants I can trust. Feng Chee will have to find other employment, or he will need to make other arrangements for his niece's care. I cannot have a common thief such as Lin Mei in my house."

"That's rotten," Jenny burst out. "Low-down and mean. I bet she didn't take the jewels, either. What would a little kid do with them?"

Miss Whitaker froze Jenny with one glance. "You would do well to remember, Jennifer Grant, where you are and to whom you are speaking. There is no place here for your disrespect and crude speech. My decisions are final. Do I make myself clear?"

Not a rustle of a skirt or a whisper was heard as the headmistress waited for Jenny's response. Andi held her breath, sorry for her friend, but glad Miss Whitaker's words hadn't been aimed at her.

When Jenny muttered an apology, Miss Whitaker's voice softened. "Do not try to understand the Oriental mind, Jennifer," she said. "They don't think as we do. I'm sure the child has her reasons for taking the case. Perhaps we can discover those reasons when she is found. Now, ladies, you are dismissed. Please assist my staff by searching your own rooms and any hallways and washrooms."

The students broke up into groups of twos and threes, whispering excitedly among themselves. A dull, weekday afternoon had been transformed into a thrilling search for a runaway thief.

Andi, however, had no desire to scour the grounds looking for Lin Mei. Her heart was heavy as she wondered where the little girl could be. She hoped Lin Mei had a few kind friends in Chinatown who would take her in and treat her better than Feng Chee had. But why had she decided to run away now of all times? Why not last year? Last month? A week ago? Although she was poorly treated, she'd never indicated to Andi that she wanted to escape. She seemed browbeaten and resigned to her fate. What had scared her into running away?

Andi turned to leave, but Miss Whitaker called her back. "Andrea, Jennifer, I'd like a word with you."

The headmistress waited until they were alone before continuing. "This entire affair is the result of your willful disregard of my instructions. Feng Chee has said as much to me as well. He holds you to blame, Andrea, for interfering with the proper order of things, both in this school and with his family." Tightly controlled anger flashed in her eyes. "I warned you the very first day to have nothing to do with the kitchen or the servants who work there. Instead of obeying my instructions, you dragged Jennifer into this business. Within a handful of days, you were caught playing with the child. Again, I warned you not to associate with Lin Mei or the other servants. I cannot understand why you do not respect my wishes."

Andi shifted uncomfortably at Miss Whitaker's scolding. She mentally began counting up disgrace marks. "All I did was show a little kindness to Lin Mei. I taught her a game. I talked to her. That's it. I never told her stories or anything else that would make her want to run away. Honest. I can't imagine why Feng Chee would blame me for anything."

"I will hear no excuses," Miss Whitaker snapped. "You have disobeyed me and as a result, the school is now embroiled in a scandal." She shuddered. Her cheeks flamed red. "Since your Aunt Rebecca is on the board, I will have to inform her of the situation. I have no idea how she and the board will react. A crime has been committed, so the police will probably be called in as well."

*The police?* Andi thought. *Oh, no!*

Miss Whitaker wadded up her handkerchief and stuffed it in her sleeve. "I have a question, and then you may go."

Andi and Jenny waited.

"Do you have any idea where the child might be hiding?"

"No, ma'am," Andi answered quickly.

"We haven't seen Lin Mei all week," Jenny added. "Wen Shu brought the linens up the other evening."

"I see. You're dismissed to join the others in the search."

Andi couldn't get away from Miss Whitaker fast enough. She stuffed her schoolbooks under her arm and hurried from the room, Jenny at her side. Together they dashed up the stairs, through the hall, and into their room. Jenny slammed the heavy door shut and leaned against it, while Andi collapsed onto her bed.

"Miss Whitaker's sure riled up," Jenny said, panting.

Andi closed her eyes and winced. "She's sure going to give Aunt Rebecca an earful. I expect I'll get a visit from Auntie real soon. I just hope she doesn't write to Mother." She opened her eyes and glanced at the calendar hanging on the wall by her bed. Large red X's covered three and a half rows of squares. "How many more weeks of this can I endure?" she wondered aloud.

Suddenly she heard quiet weeping. She pulled her gaze from the calendar. "What's wrong?"

Jenny's eyes opened wide. "Nothing."

"But you were crying."

"Not me!"

Both girls froze as a tiny hiccup sounded. They stared at each other, mouths agape. Then Andi tumbled to the floor and yanked at the bed coverings. A narrow space opened before her, dark and dusty. She could barely make out a small, shadowy lump in the corner.

Jenny shoved her freckled face next to Andi's and peered under the bed. "What is it?"

Andi met her friend's wide, uncertain eyes. She swallowed. Her heart was racing out of control. "I . . . I think we found Lin Mei."

*Chapter Ten*

# THE HIDEAWAY

Jenny yelped her surprise. Then she glanced around the room, as if the walls had ears. "What are you waiting for?" she whispered. "Let's get the poor kid out of there."

It took several minutes of quiet coaxing to convince Lin Mei to crawl out from under the bed. With whimpers and hiccups, the little girl finally allowed Andi and Jenny to lift her up on the bed and brush away the cobwebs that clung to her hair and face.

Andi caught her breath. The child's mouth, face, and hands were badly swollen. She was trembling, and her frightened gaze darted back and forth like a baby rabbit caught in a snare. In one hand she clutched a small, dirty cloth bundle.

"Please, missee," she whispered between hiccups, "not to tell." She secured the bundle inside her tunic, pulled her knees under her chin, and curled up against the wall.

"We won't tell," Jenny said. She sat down on the bed and turned to Andi. "Right?"

Andi simply stared, her heart racing. It slammed against the inside of her chest like a galloping horse. Her palms were sticky with sweat, and now her stomach had decided to get into the act. The dull, twisting ache had nothing to do with hunger. It was fear—true, gut-wrenching fear. Fear for Lin Mei, and yes, fear for herself. And for Jenny. *What should we do?* She fought to keep her hands from shaking. *If Miss Whitaker walks in and sees her runaway thief with us, she'll . . .*

"Lin Mei," she said in a hushed voice, "did you steal Miss Whitaker's jewelry?"

Lin Mei gasped and shook her head. "No. No steal jewels. Never. Run, yes. Steal, no."

"Then what's that bundle you stuffed under your shirt?"

Warily, Lin Mei straightened up. She reached inside her tunic, pulled out the scrap of fabric, and unwrapped it. A scanty assortment of items lay in a heap in the middle of the cloth: a few small, soiled garments, a broken comb, and two little wooden chopsticks. These were clearly the Chinese girl's treasures, and her only worldly possessions. When Andi nodded, Lin Mei tied up the ends of her bundle and thrust it back inside her tunic.

Andi's thoughts whirled. She knew the sensible thing was to tell Miss Whitaker the child had been found, safe and unharmed. Aunt Rebecca would expect her to cooperate, and she'd promised Juan Carlos she'd leave Lin Mei to God and let the matter go. But now? Surely Lin Mei hadn't chosen Andi and Jenny's room by accident.

"Why did you run away?" she asked.

Lin Mei started crying. Huge, wrenching sobs wracked her tiny body; a flood of tears spilled down her puffy cheeks.

Quick as a flash, Jenny reached out and gently clapped a hand over Lin Mei's mouth. "Shh! Do you want to bring the entire school in here?"

Lin Mei shook her head. When Jenny removed her hand, the little girl wept quietly and muttered in Chinese.

Although Andi didn't understand a single word, she knew it was the sound of a helpless child with no hope and nowhere to turn. Lin Mei had run away simply because she had no choice. Something terrible must have happened.

Andi scooted next to the girl and put an arm around her shaking shoulders. She pulled her close. "It's all right, Lin Mei. We won't tell. You're safe for now. Tell us why you ran away."

Lin Mei's sobs gradually turned to sniffles, which she wiped away with the back of her hand. She took a deep breath and said, "In the

night Feng Chee think I sleep. I hear talk. He talk to Chung Bow"—
her face turned terror-stricken—"Chung Bow say he buy me. Take me
far away. No more trouble for Feng Chee from nosy *fahn quai*—white
devils." She bit her lip. "He mean you, missee. You ask questions. You
not mind own business. You care about slave." She shook her head,
as if she couldn't understand why anyone would care. "That mean
trouble for Feng Chee."

"Feng Chee plans to sell you?"

Lin Mei nodded. "To Chung Bow. Chung Bow bad man. Very
bad man. He buy slaves and sell them far away—never come back to
Chinatown." Her eyes welled up with fresh tears. "You kind, missee.
You help Lin Mei. Keep Feng Chee far away."

Jenny, who had kept silent during Lin Mei's sad tale, took a deep
breath and turned to Andi. The look on her face showed how much
she wanted to scream. Instead, her words came out as a low hiss. "This
kind of tromps on that promise you made the stable boy, doesn't it?
He didn't want you dragging Lin Mei away from Feng Chee. But it
looks like Lin Mei's come to you for help. What now?"

Andi untangled herself from Lin Mei and leaned her head back
against the wall. She closed her eyes. *What now, indeed?* For a full
minute she sat there, unmoving, thinking. *If I tell Miss Whitaker Lin
Mei is here, she'll turn her over to her so-called uncle, who in turn will
sell her before she can blink. Then he'll make up some cock-and-bull story
about how she went to live with relatives. And I bet ol' Feng Chee knows
more about Miss Whitaker's jewels than he's telling. How much easier to
get the school on his side if his niece is a thief!* Her anger burned against
Feng Chee and his crafty schemes.

She opened her eyes and saw Jenny and Lin Mei watching her.
"You're right, Jenny. This changes everything. Helping Lin Mei escape
from Feng Chee now isn't breaking my promise to Juan Carlos."

"Yippee!" Jenny shrieked, then clapped a hand over her mouth.
"Sorry," she said between her fingers. The grin on her face spread clear
to her merry brown eyes.

Andi didn't feel merry at all. Juan Carlos's words from the week before echoed a warning in her head: *If you meddle in this affair, you will cause more trouble . . . Feng Chee is a dangerous man when crossed.* She shook off the warning and replaced her uncertainty with grim determination. Lin Mei needed help. She couldn't turn her over to Miss Whitaker, which meant the only other option was to help her escape from her master. But how?

As if reading her thoughts, Jenny whispered, "How are we going to get Lin Mei to safety? Where can we take her?"

Andi knew only one safe place for Lin Mei in all of San Francisco— with her sister, Kate. She didn't know if Aunt Rebecca was willing to hide a small Chinese girl—in fact she rather doubted it—but Andi knew her older sister would help her. "The problem is getting her there," she said, thinking aloud, "and then keeping her hidden so Aunt Rebecca doesn't find her."

"We're taking Lin Mei to your aunt's house?" Jenny scooted across the bed and pushed herself to her feet. "Well, what are we waiting for?" she demanded when Andi and Lin Mei made no move to follow her.

Andi put a finger to her lips. "Shh! Pacific Heights isn't just around the corner, and I'm not even sure where it is. These hills all look alike to me. Once up there, I know I could find her house, but—"

"So we ask somebody!" Jenny was clearly raring to go. She paced their small room and waved her arms to keep Andi's attention. "We've gotta go before somebody finds Lin Mei here."

Andi glanced at Lin Mei. The little girl sat crumpled against the wall, eyes half closed. She looked exhausted from terror and uncertainty. As Andi watched, her head dropped to her chest, she began to lean to one side, and then slowly she slumped onto the bed, asleep. It was perhaps the first time she'd felt safe enough to close her eyes.

"We can't leave now," Andi decided. "She's asleep. Besides, it's nearly suppertime, and we'd be missed. It's foolish to try and sneak away today or tonight, what with everybody searching the grounds. We need to wait until they get tired of looking for her." Carefully, she flipped the top quilt over Lin Mei, arranged a small bundle of clothes on either side of the lump, and carefully set her pillow on top of the mound. She put a finger to her lips and slid from the bed. "Come on, Jenny," she whispered, "she's safe for now. Nobody'll see her. We'll turn down the lights and she'll look like a pile of laundry."

"I hope you're right," Jenny said with a sigh, "'cause if they find her, she'll never get another chance to get away."

Andi drew the dark, heavy drapes across the windows. Then she fiddled with the gaslight until dark shadows settled over the room and crept into the corners. She could barely make out the small heap on her bed in the dim light.

Closing the door softly behind them, Andi and Jenny made their way through the hallway and down the wide, curved stairs. They joined a group of girls heading outside. "Has anyone checked the stables?" Andi asked. If she could talk to Juan Carlos, perhaps he could offer some advice.

Emma Banks, a cheerful girl a little younger than Andi, replied, "We're going there now. Oh, I do hope we find her. Poor Miss Whitaker! How dreadful that she's lost her precious heirlooms."

When they arrived at the stables, Juan Carlos was nowhere in sight; neither was Mr. Hunter. "They're probably searching the grounds," Emma said. She disappeared behind the rest of the group as they circled the building, leaving Andi and Jenny alone.

Jenny rested her elbows on a stall's half-door and cupped her chin in her hands. "Why do you need to talk to that stable boy?"

Andi gave the mare, Penny, an affectionate pat and peered into the stall. Penny's colt was resting in a corner, snug for the approaching chilly night. "Howdy, little fella," she called with a grin. No matter how badly things might be going, a visit with a horse always cheered Andi. She pulled her gaze from the little family. "We can't walk all the way to Aunt Rebecca's, especially with Lin Mei. We're going to need a horse. Juan Carlos can help us; he can probably tell us the easiest way to Pacific Heights." She turned back to Penny and rubbed her nose. "If he will."

A slight tightening in her gut made Andi realize that she wasn't sure if Juan Carlos would help. He'd refused once already. Would he change his mind when he learned the truth about Lin Mei's desperate situation? There was only one way to find out, but it didn't look like she'd get the chance to talk to him this evening. Dusk was creeping in, and the dinner bell would soon call them in to supper.

She spent a few more minutes idly rubbing Penny's nose, hoping Juan Carlos would magically appear. But he didn't. When the rest of the girls filed past her, Andi was forced to admit defeat and return to the school for the evening meal. She'd have to wait for tomorrow's riding lesson to ask Juan Carlos's advice.

Supper was a gloomy affair. Miss Whitaker's distress over her missing jewelry and the runaway servant girl hung over the meal like a storm ready to break. Miss Whitaker sat at the head of the table, stiff and formal; the smallest breach of table etiquette brought her sharp tongue and glaring eyes down on the offender. It was clear she was worried that this hint of scandal would somehow affect her academy's spotless reputation.

No one dared speak; the air crackled with unspoken finger-pointing. Andi felt some of it aimed at her. *If you'd just left well enough alone*, the looks seemed to be saying. *This is what happens when you don't stay in your own social class.*

The fact that Lin Mei slept only one floor away kept Andi on pins and needles. She wasn't a bit hungry. She exchanged a quick glance with Jenny, who sat across the table from her. Her friend looked as guilty as Andi felt.

By the time the meal ended, Andi was ready to lose what little food she had forced down. She'd stuffed bits of bread in her skirt pockets, along with a small chicken leg, which she knew would muck up her skirt and make it unfit to wear the next day. Each time she put her hand in her pocket, her heart gave a leap. *Surely Miss Whitaker can see how jumpy I am.*

But Lin Mei had to eat, and Andi needed time to think. She couldn't let the little girl go hungry while she was figuring out what to do. Deciding to take Lin Mei to Aunt Rebecca's was very different from actually doing it.

When the girls returned to their room after supper, Andi turned up the light a smidgen and peeked at the still-sleeping Lin Mei. The child hadn't moved an inch while they were gone. Andi pulled the supper leftovers from her pockets and laid the meager fare on the washstand. Jenny set her offerings beside the chicken leg and made a face.

"Doesn't look very appetizing," she whispered.

"I don't think Lin Mei will mind," Andi whispered back. She pulled back the bed coverings and tried to make the little girl comfortable against the wall. Then she quickly made herself ready for bed and crawled in beside her. It was a tight fit.

"You sleep with her tonight," Jenny said, climbing into her own bed, "and she can sleep with me tomorrow night."

*Tomorrow night? And what about the next night? And the night after that?* Andi lay on her back and pulled the bedclothes up to her neck. *How long will we have to hide her? How long until we get caught? How do we get her to Aunt Rebecca's?* Andi fell asleep with a dozen more questions tumbling around in her head.

She slept fitfully. She dreamed that Lin Mei was screaming, hanging on her skirt and begging Andi not to sell her. The sobs and shrieks tore at her heart; she felt smothered. With a start, she woke up to find that Lin Mei really *was* shrieking, caught in the middle of some dreadful nightmare.

Andi's heart leaped to her throat. Surely the entire household could hear the screams. Even though their room was in a corner next to the washroom, the walls were not soundproof.

Sure enough, a sudden staccato tapping on their door and Florence's frightened voice sounded. "Andrea! Jennifer! Are you all right? Whatever is the matter?"

Andi clapped her hand over Lin Mei's mouth and tried to muffle the sound. She buried her under the covers and waited. She heard a rustling, the scurrying of feet, and the creaking of the door being opened. "Oh, it was terrible," she heard Jenny cry out to Florence. "Such a terrible nightmare! But it's over. You can go on back to bed, Florence. We're fine now. But thank you for checking on us."

From her bed, Andi could see the golden glow from the hallway's lamps. It framed Florence's face as she tried to see around Jenny and into the dark room. "Are you certain?" she asked, her voice anxious. "Shall I call for Miss Whitaker?"

"Miss Whitaker has enough worries," Jenny answered. "Let's not yank her from what precious little sleep she gets." Before Florence could reply, Jenny said, "Good night," and closed the door. The room plunged into darkness.

A few minutes later, Jenny turned up the light.

"That was close," Andi whispered.

Jenny slumped on her bed and looked over at Andi and Lin Mei. Her freckles stood out against her ashen face. "At least I didn't have to lie," she said with a lopsided grin.

"Hiding Lin Mei in our room is almost like a lie," Andi mumbled. She was scared and shaken.

Lin Mei, who had recovered from her nightmare, clutched Andi's arm. "Sorry, missee. No want trouble. Sorry."

"It's not your fault," Andi assured her with a weak smile. "You're just trying to get away. We'll get you out of here one way or another. Are you hungry?"

Lin Mei nodded, and Jenny brought her the scanty meal on a small towel. The child snatched up the chicken leg and began to devour it.

"Tomorrow afternoon I'll ask Juan Carlos how to find Pacific Heights. Perhaps he'll even let us take a horse." She looked at Lin

Mei stuffing the food into her mouth. "One thing's sure, we can't keep her here much longer."

## Chapter Eleven

# A RACE AGAINST TIME

For the next two days it drizzled, and Andi's riding lessons were suspended. Since she had no good excuse to talk to Juan Carlos, the girls kept Lin Mei out of sight the best they could and waited for the weather to clear. During the day, Lin Mei huddled in a corner under Andi's bed, safely hidden away from probing eyes and unannounced room inspections. It was an uncomfortable and tedious place to stay, but she never uttered a word of complaint. Lin Mei seemed to know how uncertain her position was. She appeared grateful when Andi and Jenny brought her scraps from the table, and she ate the food with gusto. She played Cat's Cradle with the girls, but she didn't smile or giggle or chatter. She did, however, give in to Andi's pleading to share something about her past.

"I remember China," she said as the third day of hiding slipped into late afternoon. "Father owe money to gambling den." She sniffed back a few tears. "Father sell me. Mother cry. I cry. But Father not listen. He drag me from Mother and sell me to old woman. She say not to worry. I have good life in *Kum Sum*. No more poor. Good family care for me. I marry rich man." She shook her head. "All lies. She put me on big boat. Very bad place. Very sick. When boat dock, Feng Chee say I belong to him. He my uncle. But not true. He give money for me." She sighed and dropped her head. "Long time ago. Best to forget."

Andi let out the breath she'd been holding. The details of Lin Mei's short, sad life rendered her speechless. *This can't be true. Surely people don't do such things to their own children. Sell them to pay off gambling debts?* But Lin Mei had told the story so matter-of-factly that Andi had no reason to doubt her. She simply didn't want to believe it. The child had been treated like cargo and taken to a foreign land. Worked half to death, and in danger of being sold again because she might cause trouble for Feng Chee, Lin Mei had no control over her fate.

"Don't worry, Lin Mei," Andi finally said. She put an arm around her shoulder and gave her a squeeze. "Jenny and I will do everything we can to make sure Feng Chee never finds you. My sister will take care of you; there are lots of hiding places in Aunt Rebecca's house." Andi didn't know what would eventually happen to Lin Mei, but she knew they had to get her away from the school before she was discovered.

A sudden tapping on their door propelled the girls into action. They were sitting on the floor next to Andi's bed, where they'd sat each day, close to Lin Mei's hiding place. With a swiftness that astounded Andi, the little girl disappeared under the bed—just in time. Celia, the maid, poked her head in the room. "Beggin' your pardon, miss," she directed her message to Andi, "but the missus wants to see you in her office right away."

Andi's stomach flip-flopped. She exchanged a panicked look with Jenny before replying to Celia. "Do you know why she wants to see me?"

Celia opened the door wider and stepped through. "Can't say for sure, miss, but I'll tell you this. She looks fit to be tied. Never seen her so jumpy. There's something troubling her." A frown creased her forehead. "Come along quickly, miss. You don't want to make her more upset than she is."

Jenny stood up. "She doesn't want to see me? Just Andi?"

"That's what she told me, miss."

Andi rose to her feet and flicked a piece of lint from her dark blue skirt. It was a casual gesture, but her insides were swirling with anxiety. "Well, I guess there's nothing to be done but to go see what she wants. It's probably nothing, Jenny," she said when she saw her friend's worried expression.

"I wouldn't be too sure of that, miss," were Celia's parting words as she led Andi out of the room.

A few minutes later, in response to a muffled, "Enter," Andi stepped into the office. Miss Whitaker sat behind her desk. She seemed to have shrunk in size. The restless tapping of her pen on her desktop and her dark, haunted eyes told Andi that indeed, the headmistress was deeply troubled.

"You wanted to see me, Miss Whitaker?"

"Yes," she said, reaching for a piece of paper. "This won't take long." She adjusted her spectacles, glanced at the paper, and spoke without looking up. "A messenger delivered this note from your aunt. She'll be sending Thomas around in the morning to take you home—"

Andi gasped. "Home? To the ranch?"

Miss Whitaker removed her glasses and regarded Andi coldly. "Home to Rebecca's, I imagine. Allow me to finish, please."

Andi swallowed and nodded.

"It appears that your aunt wishes to distance you from"—her voice choked—"any potential scandal surrounding the school. The runaway servant, a crime taking place on the premises, the fact that I mentioned your involvement with the China girl, and . . . other matters have caused Rebecca to question my ability to shield my students from things 'which are not fitting for young girls to witness,' as she wrote in her letter." She paused, as if to collect her thoughts. "Rebecca has not wired your mother . . ."

Andi sighed. *Thank goodness!*

"But your brother Justin is arriving in the city either tonight or tomorrow, and he will no doubt look into the matter." She let the paper fall from her hand. "I'm quite sure there will be a board of inquiry."

Andi didn't know what a board of inquiry was, but Miss Whitaker didn't seem to like the idea. "Aunt Rebecca means well," Andi said, "but she worries too much about her reputation. I'm sure everything will be fine once you get your jewels back and catch the thief." For some reason, she wanted to comfort the woman. "I don't understand why she's making me go home because of it. It's a silly reason, if you ask me."

Miss Whitaker frowned. "I'm not asking you, Andrea. And you would do well not to criticize your elders." Once again, she was the headmistress Andi recognized. "The decision has been made. You will pack your things and be ready to leave when Thomas arrives in the morning." She stood up. "You're dismissed."

When Andi opened the door to her room, Jenny yanked her inside, slammed the door shut, and bombarded her with questions. "Did she eat you alive? What did she want? Does she suspect we're hiding Lin Mei? Did you earn more disgrace marks? What happened?"

Andi paid no attention to Jenny's prattling. She brushed her aside and made her way to her bed in a daze. She sat down and turned a stricken look on Jenny and Lin Mei. "I'm going to Aunt Rebecca's. First thing in the morning. Miss Whitaker told me to pack my things."

Jenny gaped at her.

"You leave?" Lin Mei burst out. "Take Lin Mei, yes?"

"I . . . I don't know. Aunt Rebecca wants me away from the school until this whole affair about Lin Mei and the stolen jewelry is settled." She slumped. "It's just like Auntie to worry about what folks might say if they learn the school's involved in a scandal. It doesn't matter how small or ridiculous it is, either. To Aunt Rebecca, what looks proper is all that counts. She'd simply die if she saw her name—with a black mark beside it—in the paper's society page." Andi threw herself backward onto her bed and stared at the ceiling. "And horror of horrors that her niece might be part of it."

For once, Jenny was speechless.

"Justin's coming to town," Andi said after a few minutes of awkward silence. She rolled onto her side and propped her head up. "He'll smooth Auntie's ruffled feathers and help with Lin Mei. I know he will. Between Justin and Kate, everything will work out. But it means we have to take her to Aunt Rebecca's today, right after supper. Or," she considered, "I could go to Auntie's tomorrow and bring Justin here. He'd—"

Jenny shook her head. "You can't go off and leave Lin Mei and me here, trapped like rats on a sinking ship." She jumped up and hurried to the room's large windows. "I've been doing some thinking the past couple days, and I came up with a plan to get us out of here unseen." She flung the drapes aside and shoved the window open. "We'll leave through the window and climb down that tree." She pointed to the giant eucalyptus next to the window.

Andi made her way to the window and looked down. She looked at the tree. Then she looked at Jenny. "You're *loco*. It's too big a stretch from here to those branches. They look scrawny besides. Can they even hold us?"

Jenny tossed her wild mane aside and slid onto the windowsill. "You might know everything there is to know about horses, Andi Carter, but I know everything there is to know about trees."

Before Andi could stop her, Jenny slipped through the window and scampered like a monkey across the branches and down the trunk of the great tree. A minute later, she was back, breathing hard, but with a wide grin on her face. She scrambled through the window and collapsed to the floor with a gasp. "What did I tell you, rancher-girl? I'll get us out of here and safely to the ground. The rest is up to you."

Andi glanced at Lin Mei, sitting on the floor. Perhaps it would be best to get her out tonight. "All right. We'll go to Aunt Rebecca's, but you'll have to hide in the yard. Auntie will scold me for showing up tonight, but once I'm free, I'll find you and sneak you inside."

The dinner bell rang.

"So soon?" Andi said in surprise.

"The sooner the better, as far as I'm concerned," Jenny said.

On cue, Lin Mei scooted under the bed to hide for what Andi hoped would be the last time.

"Is it still raining?" Andi asked Jenny an hour and a half later. Supper had dragged. When the girls finally returned to their rooms for the evening, dusk was settling over the grounds.

"Not that I can see," Jenny replied from the window. She turned around. "There's still some light. Let's go."

Andi pulled her cloak around her, snatched Lin Mei's hand, and gave it a squeeze. "Ready?"

"Not to worry," Lin Mei said. "We go far away, yes?"

Andi nodded and led her to the window. Jenny had disappeared through the opening and stood a few feet away, balancing on a wobbly branch and holding out her hand.

"Don't be afraid, Lin Mei. I won't let you drop. Grab my hand."

There was a moment of uncertainty, when Lin Mei balanced dangerously between the sill and Jenny's hand. Then she leaned forward, grasped the outstretched hand, and leaped to the safety of Jenny's arms.

"You did good, Lin Mei," Jenny assured her. Branch by branch, she guided the little girl down the tree until her feet touched solid ground. "Come on, Andi," she called up to the second-story window.

Andi had climbed her share of trees, but none quite so high and unsteady. It took all her courage to push off from the security of the solid oak windowsill to the narrow tree limbs. Once across, she scrambled down the branches and dropped to the ground with a thud.

Elated at their success so far, Andi, Jenny, and Lin Mei slipped across the clipped lawn—still wet from recent showers—and past the fountain until they reached the stables. They flattened themselves against the back side of the building and paused.

"What now?" Jenny whispered.

Andi crept toward the narrow back entrance. "Follow me." She cracked the door open and slipped through. The others hurried after her. It was dark inside, except for a pale glow coming from the far side of the stable. Andi figured it would be best to stay away from any lamp. *Where there's light, there are people*, she reasoned. *It might be Juan Carlos, but it might not.*

She led them to a nearby stall, unlatched the door, and waved them inside. A large chestnut horse snorted his surprise at the intruders. Jenny shrank back with a gasp, yanking Lin Mei with her, but Andi stood firm.

"Easy, Big Red," she crooned, patting his shoulder. "You remember me. I'm Juan Carlos's friend. We only want to share your stall a minute. What do you say?"

The horse appeared to relax. He shook his mane and nuzzled Andi affectionately.

"That's better." She turned to her friends. "Stay here while I look for Juan Carlos. He can tell us the best way to get to Pacific Heights. Maybe he'll take us there himself."

"What if he refuses to help?" Jenny asked in a harsh whisper.

"I'll explain it to him," Andi replied. She closed the half-door of the stall and backed away. "When he hears what's happened, I'm sure he'll help us. You may think he's just a stable hand and a servant, Jenny, but he's a gentleman. He won't leave Lin Mei in such a fix—or us, either."

But as Andi secured the latch and crept away, she wasn't so sure. Juan Carlos had been adamant about leaving the situation with the kitchen servants alone. Would he risk his job at the academy for the sake of a Chinese slave? A stirring of doubt made her heart flutter. *I have to take the chance. He knows the city.*

Andi made her way through the dark building. Once or twice she called out softly, "Juan, are you here? I need to talk to you," but there was no reply. She checked the corner of the stable, where a crude cot and a small table sat—Juan Carlos's tiny quarters. He wasn't there. She tiptoed past the tack room and peeked around the corner where she'd seen the light. A worktable rested directly below the hanging lantern; its surface was covered with pieces of leather, scattered tools, a mound of rags, and a half-empty whiskey bottle. It looked as if someone had been working until a few minutes ago. Now the place was deserted.

"Juan Carlos?" she whispered.

No answer.

*I don't like this*, Andi thought. *It's too quiet. Too empty.* She turned around and headed back to the stall. She felt her way along the rough boards. Light seeped through the narrow gaps near the roof, but it barely pierced the gloom.

She unlatched the stall door and threw it open. "I can't find Juan Carlos. And we don't dare wait any longer. Somebody's sure to figure out we're missing sooner or later."

Jenny groaned and stood up from the corner. "So what do we do?"

"I'll throw a bridle on Big Red and we'll leave. Then I reckon we'll do like you first suggested—ask somebody on the street how to get to Pacific Heights."

Jenny looked up at the huge horse. "We're all riding him?"

Andi ran her hand along Big Red's flank. "Yep. Bareback, astride, with Lin Mei between us. It'll be a snap."

"If you say so," Jenny said doubtfully.

Before Andi could reassure her friend, a raspy voice growled, "Well, *I* don't say so."

Andi spun around.

Mr. Hunter stood in the aisle, fists planted against his hips. "Where do you think you're going with that horse?"

## Chapter Twelve

# CHANGE OF PLANS

A wave of horror washed over Andi at the sight of the grounds-keeper's gloating, grizzled face. She clutched Big Red's mane to keep from collapsing to the ground. From the corner of the stall she heard a gasp and muffled whimpering.

"M-mister H-hunter," she stammered. Her wits were too frozen to say anything else.

"In the flesh," the man said with a sneer. He took a step forward and squinted into the dark stall. "Well, well, what do we have here? The little runaway China girl. Ain't it my lucky day! Heard tell there's a reward for finding her. I reckon ol' Feng Chee don't like the notion of his niece running off with the missus's jewels." He scratched at his stubby chin. "Don't know why a scrawny China girl would be worth a hundred bucks, but I'm happy to collect."

At Mr. Hunter's words, Lin Mei broke into a wail that echoed through the entire building. She wrapped her arms around herself and rocked back and forth, sobbing.

"You're not taking her anywhere!" Jenny yelled. She threw herself next to Lin Mei and wrapped her arms around her.

Mr. Hunter laughed. "Actually, I'm not taking any of you. I'm locking you in the stall while I find the missus and Feng Chee. But first"—he reached into a pocket of his baggy trousers and pulled out a small flask—"a drink to celebrate my good fortune."

He raised the flask to his lips and swallowed gulp after gulp.

Andi watched helplessly. There was no use trying to reason with the gruff, unfeeling lout. She knew that even if no reward were offered,

Mr. Hunter would still turn Lin Mei over to Miss Whitaker and Feng Chee.

Mr. Hunter lowered his flask, swiped at his mouth with the back of his shirtsleeve, and stuffed the bottle in his pocket. Then he reached for the two halves of the stall door. "Now, don't go anywhere, my—"

*Crash!*

Andi leaped backward at the sound and watched, mouth agape, as Mr. Hunter crumpled to the dirt floor in a heap. Juan Carlos stood over him, holding what was left of a whiskey bottle. Tossing the bottle aside, he squatted next to the fallen man. He put an ear to Mr. Hunter's chest, then rose and crossed himself. He spoke to Andi in hurried Spanish. "He's alive, *gracias a Dios*. I have never killed a man, and I do not want *Señor* Hunter to be the first, even if he is a fool and an oaf."

"Thank you," Andi said, near tears. Never had she been so glad to see her friend.

Juan looked past her into the stall. Jenny and Lin Mei huddled in a corner behind Big Red. "I thought as much," he muttered. "I heard someone cry out and came to investigate. I understood enough of *Señor* Hunter's words to know that you were in trouble. Explain, *por favor*, what you are doing here, *señorita*."

"We came to the stables to find you."

As Andi quickly told how they'd come to be in Big Red's stall, Juan Carlos's jaw dropped lower and lower. His dark gazed flicked between Andi and the Chinese girl, and occasionally came to rest on Jenny as well. "Since Lin Mei came to me for help, I figured I wasn't breaking my promise to you. I meant to ask your advice during my next riding lesson, but . . ." her voice trailed off at Juan's astonished look.

"The rain prevented your lesson, so you hid the child under your bed? A daring plan, *señorita*. It might have had some hope of success had not *Señor* Hunter interrupted you."

"We can still get Lin Mei to my aunt's. Big Red can carry us. You only need to tell us how to get to Pacific Heights, or"—she gave him a pleading look—"take us there."

Juan Carlos frowned. "That I cannot do." He nodded at the unconscious figure lying in the aisle. "*Señor* Hunter will soon wake up. He will see the missing horse, his missing prisoners, and his missing stable hand. By the time he finishes with me, I will not only have lost my position, but more than likely will also find myself in jail for horse stealing."

"I'll explain," Andi said.

Juan Carlos shook his head. "It must be you and the other *señorita*. *Señor* Hunter will rant and rave, but he will take no action against the young ladies of the school. He knows his boundaries. I, however, am not so lucky to have an influential family that can come to my rescue."

By now, Jenny and Lin Mei had risen and made their way past the horse. They came and stood beside Andi. It was clear they couldn't understand the conversation, but Jenny smiled at Juan Carlos. "Thanks." She pointed at Mr. Hunter.

Juan Carlos gave Jenny a polite bow. "You are most welcome, *señorita*," he said in passable English. Then he turned back to Andi and lapsed into Spanish. "Listen to me. There is a better place to take Lin Mei than to your aunt's. You say you must hide her there and hope your sister can keep her away from Feng Chee. But you are not sure it will turn out as you wish. The place of which I speak is nearby— just down the hill—on the edge of Chinatown. It is a mission home run by brave, God-fearing ladies who fight the yellow slave trade by rescuing girls like Lin Mei."

"Go on," Andi said.

"They keep the girls safe behind the brick walls of the mission and teach them the ways of God," Juan continued. "The Chinese slave owners hate the mission, but if Lin Mei is truly a slave, as you say, then it is the best place for her to go. If you can get her there, she will be safe—at least for the time being. The women who run it know what they're doing. They have many supporters among influential San Francisco residents."

"Where is it?" Andi asked.

"Not far. Less than a dozen blocks from here, on Sacramento Street. You don't need the horses to make this short trip, and you can be back within an hour's time, with no one the wiser."

He squatted in the dirt aisle and smoothed away the debris. Quickly, he drew a crude map with his finger. "The school is here," he said, placing a small rock on a line he had drawn. He traced his finger along the line. "You cross these streets here and here, then turn on Powell. Go along until you reach this street"—he tapped his finger in the dirt—"which is Sacramento. Follow it until you come to a large, red brick building." He rose and brushed his hands against his trousers. "I will make sure *Señor* Hunter does not wake up until after you return."

Andi gave him a puzzled look. "How will you do that?"

Juan reached down and picked up a fragment of glass. "There are more bottles where this came from," he replied with a grin. "I also intend to pour a good portion of whiskey over his clothes. Perhaps, if God is gracious, the *señor* will not remember the details of his encounter with you. He does not know who hit him, so it is possible he may think he had too much to drink and fell over." He sighed. "It is a chance we must take, but I suggest you hurry."

Andi turned to Jenny and quickly explained the change of plans. Jenny nodded her agreement, but Andi was surprised when Lin Mei began shaking her head. "No, no! No take Lin Mei to white devil house! Evil spirits there. Bad place. Please to take Lin Mei to aunt's house, missee." She clasped her hands and trembled.

"Here we go again," Jenny muttered. She rounded on Lin Mei. "Haven't you figured out that all those tales about white devils are lies to keep you and other slaves away from people who can help you?" She took the little girl's shoulders and gave her a shake. "You've got to trust us, Lin Mei. We're taking you to the missionaries, and that's that. They'll keep you safe. Understand?"

Lin Mei turned imploring eyes on Andi.

"Juan Carlos is right," Andi said. "The mission home is much closer than Aunt Rebecca's, and it's getting darker. Jenny and I can take you there and be back at the school before anyone knows we've left."

Lin Mei bowed her head and nodded. "Trust missee," she said quietly.

Together, the girls stepped out of Big Red's stall, over Mr. Hunter's still form, and back the way they'd come, toward the rear entrance. Just before Andi shoved the door open, she turned and waved to Juan. He was down on his knees, cleaning up the glass fragments near Mr. Hunter. *"Adios,* Juan Carlos, and *gracias."*

*"Vaya con Dios*—go with God. I will wait here for your return. *¡Tenga cuidado!"* he warned. "Be careful!"

*Chapter Thirteen*

# DOWN A DARK ALLEY

A ndi knew they wouldn't be safe until they were well away from the school. Dusk had fallen, and what light remained from the late winter sunset was partially hidden behind the trees and high hedges surrounding the grounds. As they passed near the old mansion, Andi could see a bright, cheery glow coming from the two large bay windows at the front of the house. No doubt a few of Miss Whitaker's scholars were practicing their pieces for the piano recital next week. With a sudden unexpected pang, Andi hoped she would be back at school in time to hear it.

Once Lin Mei was safely out of Feng Chee's reach, Andi planned to confess to Aunt Rebecca her own part in the academy's scandal. She didn't believe for an instant that Lin Mei had stolen Miss Whitaker's jewelry. With the Chinese girl safely away, perhaps Miss Whitaker could focus on finding the real thief. Andi hoped she could convince Aunt Rebecca that her precious reputation was safe. Then possibly she'd allow Andi to return to school and finish out the term, like her mother wished.

These thoughts swirled around Andi like a thick, San Francisco fog. Her head was so full of escape plans and "what ifs" that she went through the motions of walking, creeping, unlatching the wrought iron gate, and slipping through it in a daze. She was brought back to reality when Jenny asked, "Which way?"

Andi looked down the street. A few blocks away lay a world so completely foreign that it was hard to believe such a place existed in America. Was it really less than a month ago that she had stood here with Aunt Rebecca and asked what was "down there"? *Stay away from Chinatown,* Auntie's words came back to warn her. *A yellow hand will reach out and grab you. Or a trap door will open and swallow you up.*

Andi shivered. Instead of staying away from Chinatown, she was headed straight for it. She closed her eyes, imagined the map Juan Carlos had scrawled in the dirt, and started down the hill. At the end of the first block, the three girls stopped. Andi peered up at the gas lamp. There was no street sign. The lamp cast a pale glow into the deepening dusk. A block away and farther up, a streetcar clanged. "Wish we could ride," Jenny muttered. "It's chilly out here."

They'd hurried downhill and crossed two more streets when Andi cried out, "Here it is. This lamp says *Powell*." Elated that she was on the right path, she broke into a jog. Jenny and Lin Mei hurried to catch up. A block later, the Chinese girl hesitated and drew back.

Andi stopped. "What's wrong?"

Lin Mei was trembling. She looked at Andi and said, "Is true? No evil spirits?"

"I promise," Andi said. She had only Juan Carlos's word on this, but she trusted that he knew what he was talking about. "We won't leave you there unless it's perfectly safe."

Lin Mei chewed on her lip as if in deep thought. Then she drew a breath and said, "If missee speak true, then please to bring friend to mission home."

"What do you mean?" Jenny asked. "What friend?"

For a full minute, Lin Mei said nothing. The three girls stood shivering under a gaslight and waited. Finally Andi grabbed Lin Mei's hand. "C'mon. We've got to go."

"Please to bring friend," Lin Mei said in a tiny voice. "Kum Ju slave. Not far. Sell many times. Now very bad mistress. Kum Ju wash clothes. Cook food. Much work. Very much work with"—she reached a hand behind her shoulder—"baby on back. When work done for day, Kum Ju sew late for overall factory." Tears sprang to Lin Mei's eyes as she told about her friend's plight. "Please to take Kum Ju to mission home too?"

Andi stared at the little girl standing beside her. "You want us to go into Chinatown and snatch your friend away from her owner? That's a crazy notion."

"Not crazy," Lin Mei insisted. "This good time. Mistress send Kum Ju to food stalls each evening. I know where. Meet Kum Ju many times when run errands for Feng Chee. Please to come." Her dark eyes pleaded.

"In for a penny, in for a pound," Jenny said lightly. "How much trouble can another little girl be?"

"No trouble!" Lin Mei assured the girls with a glimmer of a smile. "We go fast."

"What if we get lost?" Andi said. "How will we find the mission home?" She stood her ground next to the street lamp. A few buggies creaked past, the horses clip-clopping their way over the cobblestones. The drivers didn't give the girls a second glance.

Lin Mei tugged on Andi's hand. "Not to worry, missee. Lin Mei know white devil house. Can find. Lin Mei know Chinatown. Please to follow. Find Kum Ju."

Reluctantly, Andi allowed her small friend to pull her away from the street lamp and farther toward Chinatown. A few blocks later the girls crossed the street and found themselves in the Orient. Andi's eyes opened wide. The flickering gaslights cast shadows on the pagodas, with their peaked roofs of red and black. Balconies jutted from upper stories; signs in strange, gold and black Chinese characters hung beside shops filled with goods—crates of vegetables and bins of dried meat and fish. Some were locked behind gratings as street vendors began closing up for the night.

Andi sniffed the peculiar blend of smells on the damp evening air—charcoal fires, bitter herbs, and a sickly, sweet odor she couldn't identify. She wrinkled her nose. Mingled with the odd scents rose a foul stench from the gutter. Immediately Andi coughed and drew back. Lin Mei gave her sleeve a yank. "Come, missee. Please to hurry." She clasped Jenny's hand and guided both girls through the foreign maze as easily as Andi would have jogged down the streets of Fresno.

The sharp, shrill sound of people talking in a singsong chant kept Andi spellbound as she followed Lin Mei deeper into the heart of Chinatown. Little Chinese boys in baggy trousers and long pigtails chased each other through the crowded, narrow streets, yelling and laughing. Overhead, men young and old called out and argued from the balconies. Street vendors bargained with buyers for the last sales of the evening. Live chickens squawked and flapped.

Lin Mei, clearly at home in the midst of this confusion, weaved her way through the crowd until she came to a stop in front of a noodle shop. Huge, round lanterns hung across the opening, which was cluttered with crates of fresh vegetables along the sidewalk. In a quick, lilting voice, she cried out in Chinese to the owner, who waved a thin, wrinkled arm in the opposite direction and spoke two or three sharp words.

Lin Mei shot off, dragging Andi and Jenny with her.

"What's happening?" Andi asked when Lin Mei had ducked around a corner and into a gloomy alley. The street lamps were now few and far between, and the shadows had deepened.

"Jian Hui friend," she said, panting in obvious distress. "He say Feng Chee nearby. Look all over Chinatown for me. No find. Very angry. Must hide. Please to hurry."

"Feng Chee!" Jenny gasped. "What if he shows up?"

Andi ignored her and asked Lin Mei, "What about this friend of yours? Where is she?"

"Not far," Lin Mei said. Her gaze darted back and forth along the alley. "Come."

A few minutes later, Lin Mei came to an abrupt stop near an outside stairway that led down, under the buildings.

"What's down there?" Andi asked. This was more than she'd bargained for. Nearly an hour had gone by, and it was past time to get back to the school. If Lin Mei didn't hurry, night would find them trapped in a dark, unknown part of San Francisco. She was so turned around that she would never find the mission home without Lin Mei's help.

"Kum Ju," Lin Mei said bleakly. "You wait here. I find. Not to worry."

Andi grasped the girl's tunic. "Are you sure? Maybe we should forget about Kum Ju and head for the mission home. It's getting late, and I don't mind telling you that I'm scared."

"Not to worry," Lin Mei repeated and broke free from Andi's grasp.

Andi watched the girl skitter down the stairs and into the gaping blackness. "I don't like this." She peeked over the railing and shuddered. A sour, unpleasant odor wafted up.

Jenny joined Andi at the railing. "She's sure not the scared rabbit from a week ago, is she? I guess helping her friend has perked her up some."

One minute passed. Then two. When another minute went by and Lin Mei did not appear, Jenny said, "Maybe we should go down and look for her."

"Wild horses couldn't drag me into that deep, dark hole," Andi said. "Maybe she got caught."

Andi sucked in her breath. "Don't even think such a thing!"

Less than a minute later, Lin Mei emerged from the basement, clasping the hand of a small girl perhaps a year younger than herself. At the sight of Andi and Jenny, the child cried out and drew back.

"White-devil fire hair," Lin Mei explained, pointing to Jenny's mop of red tangles. "Not to worry." She turned to the girl and spoke rapidly in Chinese.

Kum Ju nodded and looked at Andi.

"Hello," Andi said, smiling. "It's nice to meet you." She reached out and took Kum Ju's hand. It was rough and calloused like an old woman's. Her pinched face and bleary eyes told their tale of suffering.

All of a sudden, Andi was glad Lin Mei had talked her into finding Kum Ju.

She turned to Lin Mei. "Let's get out of here. You know the way to the mission home?"

"This way. Not far. Please to hurry."

The four girls set off, Lin Mei in front, with Kum Ju, Andi, and Jenny following close behind. Lin Mei dodged carts and yapping dogs and slipped into yet another murky alley.

Andi gave Jenny a worried look. "I hope Lin Mei knows where she's going," she said.

The passageway was narrower than the last alley, and crowded with Chinese men lingering in front of dark, gaping doorways. Stairways rose to second and third stories and descended to deep basements underground.

"They're staring at us," Jenny hissed at Andi. "They give me the shivers."

"I don't think this is the part of Chinatown most visitors see," Andi replied. She prodded Lin Mei. "Go faster."

They broke into a run, but just as they reached the end of the alley, Lin Mei fell to the ground with a shriek. Feng Chee stood like a dragon, blocking their way. Three angry-looking men fanned out behind him. Feng Chee snatched Lin Mei up and pointed to Andi, Jenny, and Kum Ju. A stream of Chinese poured from his mouth.

Andi gasped. She grabbed Jenny's hand and turned to flee. Before she'd run a dozen feet, strong, wiry arms shot out and grabbed her. She yelped. A hand clapped over her mouth. She tried to bite her captor's fingers. It was no use. Kicking and struggling, she was dragged to Feng Chee and slammed to the ground. Jenny fell next to her. She saw Kum Ju securely held by another man.

Feng Chee grasped Andi by the hair and gave it a yank. He brought his leering, sallow face close to hers. "No more trouble from you, missee. I see to that very soon." He straightened up and spoke a few words of Chinese to his companions.

The men yanked Andi and Jenny to their feet and spirited them down the steps into a deep, dank basement. The last thing Andi remembered was Jenny's sharp cry.

Chinatown had swallowed them up.

## Chapter Fourteen

# No Hope

A ndi woke with a dull headache and a throat as dry as cotton. She opened her eyes to darkness. She tried to sit up, but a hand clutched her arm and yanked her back to the dirt floor.

"Lie still," a familiar voice hissed in her ear. "Maybe they'll think we're still asleep."

"What?" Andi felt groggy. She turned her head and saw Jenny's face close to her own. A single candle sputtered a few feet away, but the rest of the room was inky black. Beside her lay the two little Chinese girls, their eyes closed. Beyond the candle and through the dark outline of a doorway, a kerosene lantern illuminated a small group of arguing men. They gestured angrily at each other and spoke in clipped, harsh tones.

Andi shoved Jenny's hand aside and struggled to sit up. A wave of dizziness washed over her, but she fought against it and pushed herself against the rough wall. She swallowed and tried to clear her head. It was like waking up when she'd been ill a few years ago with scarlet fever. The doctor had given her a dose of laudanum, and she had felt just like this. What was going on? She brushed her tangled hair away from her face, took a deep breath, and groaned.

"What happened?"

"I think they drugged us," Jenny said. She sat up beside Andi and wrapped her arms around her knees. "I don't remember anything after being yanked down that dark hole, but I think we're someplace else." She shivered. "Which is probably just as well. It stunk worse than a privy down there."

Andi's memory of the evening slowly returned: sneaking out of their room, leading Lin Mei to the mission home, being talked into rescuing another little slave. Hurrying through the maze of Chinatown, waiting for Lin Mei, the narrow alley . . .

*Feng Chee!* Her mind snapped awake. She looked around wildly. It was dark, but Jenny was right. This wasn't the same place they'd been taken originally. The stale, damp air smelled like ages-old rotting crates mixed with tobacco, but it was free from the stench that had nearly overwhelmed Andi when she'd been hauled down the deep stairwell that led under the street.

"Where are we?"

"I'm not sure," Jenny replied, "but I think we're in the basement of a warehouse." She wrinkled her nose. "I've seen plenty of warehouses along the waterfront in Tacoma. They all smell musty and old, with hints of what's being stored there." She shook her head. "I don't think we're in Chinatown."

That suited Andi fine. She never wanted to see Chinatown again. She rubbed her eyes and focused on the two girls beside her. With a gentle hand, she reached out and shook Lin Mei. "Are you all right?"

Lin Mei's eyes flew open at Andi's touch. The little girl latched onto Andi and buried her head in her shoulder. "Very bad, missee. Evil spirits here."

Before Andi could reply, the men's voices grew louder. She watched as one of them picked up the lantern and headed in the girls' direction. Shadows leaped up the walls and across the arched ceiling from the glow of the lamp. To Andi, the figures looked like giants approaching.

She caught her breath in surprise. Along with Feng Chee and another Chinese stood two men who looked like American sailors. The one holding the lantern crouched on the dirt floor and brought the light close to the girls. Dirty, straggly hair hung over a face covered by the stubble of a beard. He wore shabby, pinstriped trousers tied with a belt of rope and a jacket that had once been white.

"Who are you?" Jenny demanded in a shaking voice.

A smile cracked the sailor's face. "Somebody interested in seeing you safely to your destination."

For an instant, hope leaped in Andi's heart. The Americans were rescuing them! A moment later, her hopes crashed. The sailor stood and faced Feng Chee. "You gotta make it worth my while. I'm used to smuggling China girls *into* the States, not smuggling white girls *out.*" He opened his hand.

Feng Chee reached into a silk purse at his waist and lifted out a handful of gold coins. One by one, the coins dropped into the sailor's palm, clinking as they fell together. The second sailor's eyes gleamed at the sight of the gold.

"Not enough," the big man growled when the coins stopped falling. "If you want 'em to disappear for good, it's gonna cost more than this." He waved at Lin Mei and Kum Ju cowering next to Andi and Jenny. "If you want the China girls to disappear too, it'll cost even more."

Feng Chee shook his head. "No. Keep slaves here tonight. I take in morning. Have buyer in San José. No trouble." He dropped a half dozen more coins into the large, rough hand then tied the purse tightly before returning it to his waistband. "No more."

The sailor jingled the coins in his hand before slipping them into his pocket. "It's a deal, Chinaman. These two"—he waved a careless hand in Andi and Jenny's direction—"go out on the morning tide. You do what you want with the others."

Feng Chee gave the sailor a curt bow, signaled to his companion, and disappeared beyond the wide opening. Soon the two Chinese were swallowed up in the dark.

"Good riddance," the gruff sailor muttered. He squatted next to the girls and leered. "You're in for a real treat, my lovelies—an extended sea voyage to the exotic Orient."

Andi shrank back against the cold, rough brick wall of the warehouse basement. A huge, cold fist seemed to squeeze her stomach. Her mind screamed, *This can't be happening!* "B-but why?" she managed to stutter. "We haven't done anything to you. Let us go.

Please. Feng Chee paid you plenty. He'll never know if you let us go."

"Let you go?" The other sailor—a short, squat man in filthy sailor pants—laughed and nudged his partner. "That's a good one, ain't it, Roy?" He reached down and snatched a handful of Andi's thick, dark hair. "Do you know how much you two is worth? A couple o' white girls in China?" He whistled. "More than the two of us can make in a year at sea."

"A chance like this don't come but once in a lifetime," Roy agreed. His grin widened. "You tangled with the wrong Chinaman, pretty girl. You helped his slave run away." As he spoke, the sailor nodded toward Lin Mei and Kum Ju, who were desperately trying to be invisible. "You got any idea what that means?"

Andi shook her head.

"A slave owner in Chinatown will pay three or four times the amount of money he paid for a slave to get her back. Otherwise he loses face. He can't let a slave get away with running off." He laughed. "Nope. Feng Chee and others like him will do anything to get their slaves back. However long it takes. However much it costs." He brought his face close to Andi's. The reek of whiskey made her cough. "I don't cross Chinamen like Feng Chee. I work for 'em. If he says you gotta disappear, then that's what I aim to do."

Jenny clenched her fists and shouted, "You'll never get away with this, you dock rats! We won't go aboard any ship quietly. We'll holler until every policeman in San Francisco hears us. They'll come running so fast it'll make your heads spin."

Roy barked a short laugh and slapped his knee. Then he rose from the ground. "You leave that to us, girlies. When the tide goes out tomorrow morning, you'll be on a ship bound for China, mark my words." He brushed his hands against his trousers. "We ain't exactly amateurs. We've shanghaied plenty of unsuspecting seamen and landsmen in our time. A couple new sailors for the crew of the

*Pacific Queen* won't pose no problems. We just have to find the right size clothes for you."

*Shanghaied?* Andi had never heard that word before. She looked at Jenny, whose face had turned white as chalk. "What do they mean? What's 'shanghaied'?"

Jenny clutched Andi's hand. "A couple years ago, my brother nearly got himself shanghaied in Portland. He told me all about it. Ruffians kidnap men on the waterfront by knocking 'em out with drugs. Next thing the poor fools know, they're on their way to the South Seas—or worse—and forced to become sailors."

Roy crossed his arms over his chest and snickered, clearly enjoying Jenny's frightened recital. "Yep, they disappear clean as a whistle—just like you two are gonna."

Jenny started shaking. "These low-down, stinking dock rats will drug us like they did before and we'll wake up on board a ship. Our families will never know what's become of us." She bit her lip and squeezed her eyes shut.

Andi threw her arms around Jenny and pulled her close. "We're not aboard any ship yet," she said. "There's got to be a way out of here."

Roy's harsh laughter startled Andi into looking up into his sneering face. "Nope. Ain't no way out of this warehouse, pretty girl. This here's a back storeroom, which I'll lock up tight when I leave. The walls are brick. You can holler and scream and carry on all you like, but nobody'll hear you. Go right ahead, if it makes you feel better." He picked up the lantern and winked. "I'll see you lovely ladies in the morning."

Andi watched as the only source of steady light began to melt into the shadows. Her heart raced at the thought of being left in the dark. "Leave us the lantern. Please!"

Roy stopped and turned. "You don't need no light. Get some sleep. You got a long voyage ahead." Then he seemed to change his mind. He reached into his jacket pocket and pulled out a small, waxy cylinder. "Here, I'll leave you an extra candle." He tossed it in Andi's lap.

She snatched it up and held it near the burning wick of the old candle stump. The new flame sprang to life. Hand trembling, she thrust it into the waxy mess on the floor. The candle did little to light up the storeroom.

The creak and rattle of the heavy wooden door yanked Andi's attention from the candle. She balled her fists and slammed them into her lap to keep them from shaking. She set her jaw. *I will not cry. It's cold and dark, but there's nothing to be afraid of. I've been locked in a shed before.*

Her brave thoughts didn't help. She brushed away the sudden, stinging tears and stared at the tiny flame through blurred eyes. *Oh, God*, she prayed, *what are we going to do?*

The sound of a padlock latching brought a sharp cry from the two little Chinese girls. "What we do, missee?" Lin Mei wailed, clutching Andi's arm. "What we do?"

Andi had no idea what they were going to do. She was so scared, she could scarcely breathe. But right now, the basement of a warehouse along the San Francisco waterfront posed less of a threat than what awaited them in the morning. "For the moment, we're safe," she said, although she felt far from safe. "Feng Chee's gone. The sailors left. We've got time." She scooted back against the brick wall and allowed Lin Mei and Kum Ju to snuggle close. It was good to feel the warmth of the girls' small, trembling bodies next to hers.

"Time?" Jenny's voice cracked. "Time for what? That candle won't last but a few minutes, and then it'll be pitch black." She began to cry in earnest. "I don't want to go to China. I want to see my mother and father again. And my brothers." Her sobs rose, and with her crying came renewed wailing from the little girls.

A wave of hopelessness washed over Andi at Jenny's words. It would be so easy to give in and let the tears come. She blinked. If she were alone, that's probably what she would do. But she wasn't alone. There were four of them—no, five when she included God—and they could make plans. Maybe the plans wouldn't work out, but anything was better than sitting in the dark, waiting for terrible things to happen to them.

Andi glanced at Jenny and the others. It didn't look like they'd stop weeping anytime soon.

*I guess it's up to me.*

## Chapter Fifteen

# A Long, Dark Night

A ndi let her friends cry for a few more minutes. Then in a loud voice, she said, "Stop it!" She picked up the candle, which was quickly melting away, and rose to her feet. "I'm scared too," she said when the wails had quieted to whimpers and hiccups, "but we can cry later. If Jenny and I find ourselves bound for China, and you and Kum Ju find yourselves with new masters, that'll be reason enough to cry. But right now, let's see what's here. Maybe there's another exit. Some stairs. *Anything.* We won't know unless we look."

Clearly heartened at the common sense in Andi's voice, Jenny stood. Lin Mei shook her head and curled up closer to Kum Ju, who looked bewildered.

"Tell her what I said," Andi ordered.

Lin Mei whispered a few words to her companion but remained curled up by the wall. "I stay with Kum Ju."

With a sigh, Andi motioned Jenny to join her. They circled the storeroom, which didn't take long. It was small, and piled high with sealed crates and solid, heavy-looking barrels. Coils of rope lay piled in a corner. There appeared to be only one door in or out.

Andi held the candle as high as she could, but the arched ceiling disappeared into shadows. No trap doors to the upper levels. Nothing but four sturdy walls, a strong, locked door, and one small candle. Her stomach clenched. *This is bad.*

"Now do you understand?" Jenny whispered. Her lip quivered. "We're trapped."

Andi gritted her teeth. She hadn't really expected to find a secret passageway or forgotten door. Storerooms were constructed to keep thieves out or—she cringed—prisoners in. But the searching had its desired effect. No one was crying.

With a sinking feeling, Andi led the way back to the little girls. She carefully lowered the candle to its spot on the floor and wondered how long it would take before everything went black.

Instead of crying, the girls silently watched the tiny flame as the candle melted lower and lower. *It won't be long now*, Andi thought. Aloud she said, "I wonder if Miss Whitaker has missed us yet."

"What difference does it make?" Jenny said. "She doesn't know where we are."

"But Juan Carlos knows where we were headed. He must know by now that we never made it back to the school. Perhaps he told Miss Whitaker what happened."

Jenny grunted. "The stable boy doesn't speak English, remember?"

"He speaks a little. He could make her understand." Andi scowled. "I wish you'd stop calling him the 'stable boy.' His name is Juan Carlos, and he's smart and kind. He's also a—"

Andi's words were cut off as the flame sputtered and died. The room plunged into darkness so black that she couldn't see her fingers in front of her face. She caught her breath and held it, mostly to keep from screaming.

Lin Mei shrieked her terror, and Kum Ju joined in. They were inconsolable as they wailed and mumbled in Chinese. Andi felt them cowering next to her. Jenny clutched her arm and said, "I'm scared of the dark."

"Who isn't?" Andi snapped. Her terror rose another notch. "All this screaming and blubbering makes it even scarier." She clutched a small body and began to shake her. "Stop it! It's dark, but we're all right. The dark can't hurt us."

"Dark *can* hurt us, missee. Evil spirits here," Lin Mei sobbed. "In dark. In corners. Every place. Evil spirits here."

"No, they're not," Andi insisted, more to convince herself than the two frightened children. "God won't let them stay. He's bigger than any evil spirit."

Her words caused Lin Mei's sobs to subside. She heard her mutter to Kum Ju, who became quiet. "What name?"

"Name?" Andi asked. She strained to see Lin Mei's face through the shroud of darkness that seemed to be suffocating her, but she couldn't see a thing.

"Name of god bigger than evil spirits."

Andi thought for a moment, then said, "Jesus."

"Jesus-God bigger? You promise?" Lin Mei sounded interested. Her small fingers dug into Andi's arm. She was grasping for a lifeline, and Andi's words brought her a flicker of hope.

"I promise," Andi said. "I've been locked in a shed before—about a year ago. I was so scared I thought I would die. I was alone. At least I thought I was. But I wasn't. You know what made me feel less frightened?" She didn't wait for a response. "I prayed, and God made me feel like He was right there with me. Like now."

Silence greeted her answer. Andi could hear the girls' quick, frightened breaths, but at least they weren't shrieking any longer. She felt a hand on her shoulder. "Keep talking," Jenny whispered in her ear. "I haven't gone to Sunday school much, so you probably know more about God than I do. You're keeping them quiet anyway." A pause. "And your words are helping me too. I don't like thinking about evil spirits lurking in this horrid place."

Andi swallowed her own fear and nodded. Then she remembered that Jenny couldn't see her. "I'll try," she whispered back. Louder, she said, "There's a story in the Bible—that's God's Book," she said for Lin Mei's benefit, "about two men named Paul and Silas who were trapped in a prison pretty near as black as this place. You know what they did?"

"No," Jenny piped up. "What did they do?"

"They prayed to God and sang songs. Then an earthquake came

along. Not that I'd want an earthquake to happen while we're under so many bricks," Andi said quickly, "but they did get free." She paused and waited for Lin Mei to relate the story to Kum Ju.

"Go 'head," Jenny said, "sing a song."

Andi's mind went blank. She hadn't planned on singing any songs. "I d-don't know if I can," she stammered.

"Please, missee," Lin Mei pleaded.

Kum Ju said something in Chinese and yanked on Andi's sleeve. Lin Mei translated. "Kum Ju say you sing or tell more story."

*What should I sing, God?* The words and melody to a popular new Sunday school song popped into her head. With a quivering voice and singing slightly off-key, Andi made her way through three verses of "What a Friend We Have in Jesus." By the time she finished the last line, her voice was strong and unwavering.

"I don't know that one," Jenny admitted. "It's nice. I do feel a mite better."

"Your Jesus-God strong," Lin Mei said. She snuggled up close to Andi. "If mission home teach this God, I go there, learn more."

Andi didn't reply. Silent, unbidden tears welled up in her eyes at the thought that Lin Mei and Kum Ju might never see the mission home. Worse, there was a good chance that she—Andi Carter—might never see her family again. Or ride Taffy. Or fish in the creek up at her special spot. Instead, she'd find herself in a strange, foreign land as a slave. Like never before, she understood what terrible sadness and hopelessness Lin Mei and Kum Ju had suffered. It had happened to them; it could happen to her. *And Mother will never know what became of me.* Silent tears streamed down her face.

Jenny's voice startled her. "Those fellas in the Bible sang. They prayed too. You've gotta say a prayer, Andi."

Andi didn't know how she'd do that without giving away the fact that she was crying.

"Pray to Jesus-God," Lin Mei insisted.

She made it quick and short. "We know you're here, God. We

know you can take care of us, but please show us how to get out of this terrible place. Amen."

After that, the darkness didn't seem so scary. The girls huddled together to wait out the long night. One by one, the others drifted to sleep, but Andi didn't close her eyes. She stayed awake and tried not to think about what would happen in the morning.

*Chapter Sixteen*

# DAWN OF HOPE

The tingling of a thousand pins and needles woke Andi with a start. Cramped in one position all night, with Lin Mei's weight crushing her, it was no wonder her legs had fallen asleep. She shook her stinging legs and yanked them out from under the sleeping child. Lin Mei grunted, sat up, and rubbed her eyes.

Andi gasped. She could see Lin Mei. True, she was only a faint, gray shadow against the dark wall, but she could see her. Frantically, Andi flicked her gaze around the storeroom. There, in the far corner, high overhead, a small square of feeble light pierced the gloom of the basement.

Andi jumped up with a shout. "It's a window! Wake up, Jenny. There's a window near the ceiling." When Jenny joined her, she pointed. "In the corner."

Jenny's jaw dropped. "Our way out was here the whole time. We just couldn't see it."

Andi nodded. "It must be dawn. But I don't know how early or late it is. The men might come back any moment. If we're getting out of here, we've got to go *now*." She glanced back at Lin Mei and Kum Ju. The girls were standing, hands clasped. They stared at the square of light with eager, expectant eyes.

"Your Jesus-God very powerful," Lin Mei murmured, shaking her head in awe.

"We're not out of here yet," Andi reminded them. She hurried over to the corner and looked up. The narrow window mocked her from nearly ten feet above. The brick walls, although rough and worn, offered no hand- or footholds.

Jenny came alongside Andi and whistled. "That's quite a climb. How do you plan to get up there?"

"This is a storeroom. There are crates and barrels here. Maybe we can move them under the window and stack them up. We sure as shootin' have got to try!" Andi found a barrel about chest-high and gave it a shove. It didn't move. "Try a different one," she said to Jenny. Even Lin Mei and Kum Ju sprang into action. However, all of the dozen or so barrels seemed to be filled with rocks.

"What if we open a barrel and try to lighten the load?" Jenny suggested.

Andi shook her head. "No time. It's getting lighter by the minute. Let's try moving one together." With much heaving and shoving, the girls managed to inch a barrel under the window. Jenny leaped to the top and reached for the window sill.

"I can't reach the ledge," she said, jumping down. "We need more height."

"Hurry," Andi said, "let's try setting a crate on top of the barrel." To her relief, the crates didn't weigh as much as she feared. Jenny and Andi easily lifted one onto the barrel. Then they eased a second crate onto the first, stretching on tiptoes to balance it.

"That's as high as we can reach," Andi said. "Besides, it doesn't look very steady. Do you want to try it or shall I?"

"I'll do it," Jenny said. "I'm taller. Find me something heavy to break the window, and hand me some of that rope." She pointed to the heavy coil lying in the corner. "It might be best if I pull Lin Mei and Kum Ju up. I can't see them climbing this heap of lumber."

Andi helped Jenny tie the rope around her waist. "You ready?"

Jenny looked at the barrel and two crates stacked next to the wall. "Ready as I'll ever be. This can't be much harder than climbing a pesky tree." She grinned and accepted the short metal rod Lin Mei thrust at her. "This'll do." She tucked it into the waistband of her skirt. "Give me a leg up."

Andi helped steady Jenny as she crawled to the top of the crates. "It's a mite wobbly," she said when she reached the top. She rose from her hands and knees and steadied herself against the wall. "I can see outside. The window opens onto an alley. It looks deserted. Here goes . . ."

A sharp *whack*, along with the crashing of glass, told Andi that Jenny had shattered the window. Then came the sound of more tinkling and crashing, and Jenny's voice. "This blamed window is so narrow, we'll cut ourselves to pieces if I don't widen it some. Look out!"

Andi and the little girls jumped back as a shower of glass fragments rained down and the metal rod dropped with a clunk at their feet.

Jenny kicked and scooted and boosted herself over the sill and through the basement window. It looked like a tight fit. Her feet disappeared, along with a good portion of the rope. A few minutes later her cheerful, freckled face popped through the opening. "I tied the rope around a post. Send the girls up."

"All right!" Andi shouted. *Thank you, God!* She motioned Lin Mei and Kum Ju to her. "Hang on tight to the rope, and Jenny will pull you up. It will be easier if you use your feet to steady yourself against the wall. Think you can do that?"

Lin Mei looked up at the high window and swallowed. She looked at Kum Ju. Then she looked at Andi. "Yes, missee. Can do. *Must* do." She wrapped her hands around the rough rope.

Andi led her to the wall and called to Jenny, "Pull her up."

It took less than a minute for Jenny to pull Lin Mei up and through the basement window to safety. Then she tossed the end of the rope down. Kum Ju, though plainly frightened, took hold of the rope as soon as Andi gave it to her.

For an instant, Andi wondered about Kum Ju. Did the weak, withered little slave have enough strength to hang on to the rope? If she let go and fell to the floor, she could be badly injured. "I have an idea," she said aloud.

She took the rope from Kum Ju and tied it into a lasso. Then she looped it over Kum Ju's head and tightened it securely under her arms. Andi guided the little girl's hands around the rope and squeezed. Hopefully Kum Ju would understand her gesture to hang on. "Pull her up!" Andi called to Jenny.

Kum Ju disappeared up and over the ledge.

The rope tumbled through the narrow opening and landed at Andi's feet. She grabbed it, then paused and looked up. Her heart fluttered. *What if Jenny's not strong enough to pull me up? What if my feet slip?*

"What are you waiting for?" Jenny called down at her.

"You're sure the rope's tied real tight around that post? I'm a lot heavier than Lin Mei."

"I'm sure. Come on!"

"I'm going to climb onto the crates first. That way you won't have to pull me so far."

Using the rope to steady herself, Andi cautiously found a toehold and boosted herself onto the rim of the barrel. She clutched the rope and continued her climb. *How did Jenny do this without falling on her face?* Admiration for her gutsy friend rose a notch.

Jenny's smile greeted Andi as she stood atop the crate. "You're nearly done."

"How am I supposed to squeeze through this narrow opening?" Andi asked.

"It's a tight fit, but your cloak will protect you. I did it. You can too." She reached out a hand. "Grab my hand and I'll—"

"Oh, no! They're coming. I hear them rattling the door." Andi leaped from the crate and clung to the window sill. "Hurry! Pull me through." Jenny clawed at her. Lin Mei and Kum Ju lent their small strength. She felt herself dangling in midair. Then the storeroom door crashed open, and she gasped. "Pull faster!" She heard a surprised shout and a curse. She knew that in seconds a huge, rough hand would curl around her ankle and yank her back.

Andi winced as her face and hands scraped the broken edges of the window. Then she was free . . . for the moment. Ignoring the pain, she staggered to her feet and brushed the broken pieces of glass from her clothes. "They'll be after us in no time. Let's go!"

Clasping hands, the girls scrambled down the alley and into a foggy San Francisco dawn.

## Chapter Seventeen

# ON THE RUN

The fog was their friend. It closed in around the runaways and muffled the sound of their feet clattering against the cobblestones as they quickly left the alley behind. Andi heaved a sigh of relief.

It was short-lived. The fog would deaden the sound of the sailors' footsteps too. She motioned her friends to halt, and listened hard. Distant shouts from the alley they'd just left sent a wave of fear through her, and she whispered, "Hurry! We're not safe yet!"

They darted in and out of a fleet of wagons, carts, and early morning street traffic. A milkman's cart with its huge tin jugs swerved to avoid hitting them. The girls dodged peddlers setting up their handcarts for the day. The sight of peanuts and oranges for sale brought a sharp pang to Andi's stomach, but she gave the food no more than a passing glance. Hunger was not as important as safety. Besides, she had no money.

Andi sniffed the sharp, salty tang of the ocean and knew they had reached the waterfront. The added stench of fish—fresh and rotten—didn't help her grumbling stomach. She slowed her pace and glanced over her shoulder. Jenny was close by, but Lin Mei and Kum Ju had fallen behind. When had she let go of their hands?

Jenny caught her arm and wheezed, "We've got to rest. The little girls are going to keel over if we don't."

Andi stopped in the middle of a busy sidewalk and gave Jenny a quick nod. "But not for long. We need to keep moving." The fog, curling and sifting through the streets, had lifted enough to reveal buildings. She pointed to an alcove wedged between a newsstand and a fruit seller. A scruffy-looking boy squatted on the sidewalk in front, stuffing newspapers into a satchel. "Let's rest over there, behind that newsboy."

Lin Mei and Kum Ju caught up, and together they crossed the street. They dodged the dark-haired boy and ducked under the arch of a three-story building, shivering and uncertain.

Andi pulled her cloak more securely around her shoulders. Now that she had stopped to rest, she noticed a throbbing pain in her cheek. She reached up and rubbed it. To her surprise, she pulled back two fingers sticky with blood.

"Sorry," Jenny said with a grimace, "you got scraped on the way out. In fact, you look like something the cat scratched up and dragged in."

Andi wiped her fingers against her skirt. She'd worry about her injuries later. "You're not the picture of refinement yourself, Miss Grant." She grinned. The realization that they'd escaped a terrible fate made her minor injuries and growing hunger pale by comparison. It was such a relief to be away from their prison that she couldn't help it. She giggled. "We look like riffraff."

For a few minutes, the girls crouched in their hiding place and gloried in the fact that they were free. They were penniless, far from home, and certainly lost, but they weren't aboard the *Pacific Queen*, headed for the Orient, and Lin Mei and Kum Ju were safe. The cheerful shout of the newsboy calling out the morning's headlines added to Andi's sense that everything would soon be well.

But as the minutes dragged by and nobody spoke or made plans, Andi's high spirits began to droop. Being lost in a city of over 200,000 was not a cheery thought. She knew Justin had a law office somewhere in San Francisco, but she didn't know where—or if he'd arrived in the city yet. She knew she could find Aunt Rebecca's if she could just figure out which of these streets led up to Pacific Heights, but she didn't have a nickel to ride the cable car. *And it's a long walk.*

As if she could read Andi's thoughts, Jenny broke the now-gloomy silence. "We're not out of the woods yet, you know."

"I know." Wearily, Andi rose to her feet. "We can't stay here, but I don't know which way to go. All the streets look alike."

"Are we going to try and find the mission home?" Jenny asked.

Andi shuddered. "We can't go back to Chinatown. Not now. We have to go to Aunt Rebecca's."

"Maybe the time's come to ask for help," Jenny suggested. "Let's find a policeman and tell him what happened. A policeman will know the way to your aunt's house. Maybe he'll arrest those dock rats too."

It was tempting. Andi need only tell a policeman her aunt's name and where she lived, and she'd be home in no time—safe, warm, and fed. Jenny, too, would find a welcome. Aunt Rebecca would notify the school of their safe return. But . . .

"What about Lin Mei and Kum Ju?" Andi asked. She already knew the answer. It wouldn't take long for the police to discover that Lin Mei was accused of stealing from the school. They'd learn that Kum Ju had run away from owners who would grieve and cry and insist they were her rightful parents. And who could prove otherwise? No policeman—or court for that matter—would take the word of any Chinese girl.

Jenny sighed. "The police'll snatch 'em quicker than scat and give 'em back to their masters, and everything we've gone through will be for nothing."

"That's what I was thinking," Andi agreed. "So no police. We stick to the original plan: take them to Aunt Rebecca's and hide them until I can talk to Justin. He'll figure something out." She gazed out into the street.

"Which leaves us exactly where we were two minutes ago," Jenny said sourly, "lost and—"

Andi caught her breath and flattened herself against the inside of the arch. "I see those sailors. They're across the street. Get down. Don't move." Jenny and the little girls fell back into the shadows.

Andi peeked around the corner and watched as the men crossed the street and turned into an alley a few yards from their hiding place. She let out the breath she was holding and relaxed. "They're gone," she told Jenny.

"I wouldn't let my guard down yet, if I was you."

Andi spun around. The newsboy stood a few feet away, with a sack of papers slung over his shoulder. His dark hair curled around his ears and stuck out from under a worn cap. He gave his tattered britches a hike up and jerked his thumb toward the alley. "How did a pretty girl like you get tangled up with the likes of them? They're a couple of ruffians."

Andi flushed. She knew she looked far from pretty this morning. "It's a long story."

"I saw you duck under the arch, and I've been keepin' an eye on you ever since. You're scared, and I bet it has something to do with *them*." He nodded toward Lin Mei and Kum Ju. "You'd best find a better place to hide. Roy and his pal will be back. Follow me."

Andi and Jenny exchanged a wary glance.

The boy sighed. "You ain't got time to decide if you can trust me or not. My name's Freddie. My folks run a hash house a few blocks away. You can rest there. What do you say?"

"I say yes," Andi blurted before she could change her mind. "My name's Andi, and it's a pleasure to meet you, Freddie. This is Jenny and Lin Mei and Kum Ju. And . . . we're on the run." In a few quick sentences she told Freddie what had happened.

Freddie whistled. "You got plenty of gumption, just like the missionary lady over at the Home. She's got more gall than a burglar, rescuing those China girls." Then he grew sober. "Come on, before those ruffians get tired of searching the alley. We'll give 'em a run for their money."

Freddie set a quick pace. He threaded his way through the multitude of San Franciscans gathered at the docks to meet an incoming ship, and he slipped by vendors hopping off and on their wagons to hawk their wares. He stopped often to sell papers, then waved the girls on. He looked to Andi like the Pied Piper of Hamelin. *And we're his rats*, she thought with a smile. *At least he's leading us away from the waterfront.*

Freddie came to a stop in front of a tiny, hole-in-the-wall restaurant and dropped his satchel to the ground. The smell of flapjacks and sizzling bacon drifted out from the open doorway. "The place ain't fancy, but you can rest here. You look done in. I'll rustle you up a square meal."

"No . . . no, we can't," Andi said, swallowing hard. "You've been a great help, but we need to get home. If you'll just point us in the direction of Pacific Heights, we'll be on our way."

Freddie gaped. "You're from up there? That's a fair distance, and uphill most of the way. You'd best take the cable car."

"Are you going to lend us money for the fare?" Jenny asked.

"Jenny!" Andi whirled on her friend. "Don't be rude. Freddie's done enough already. We can walk."

Jenny groaned.

Freddie looked embarrassed. "I'm a little short of money, but you can't walk—not with them." He pointed at Lin Mei and Kum Ju, who appeared to be wilting where they stood. "They ain't got enough sand in 'em to walk two steps, much less a couple of miles." He pulled at his lip and studied the sidewalk, deep in thought.

While Andi waited patiently for her new friend to come up with a plan, she allowed her gaze to travel up and down the street. Freddie's hash house fit in perfectly with the rest of the neighborhood, which, Andi noticed, wasn't exactly Nob Hill. Shabby carriage shops, stables, laundries, and saloons lined both sides of the avenue. Here and there, a few run-down boarding houses mixed in with small, ramshackle dwellings.

Freddie broke the silence. "I don't know what you're going to do with those two up on Pacific Heights"—he waved a careless hand at Lin Mei and Kum Ju—"but it'd be smarter to take 'em to the mission home."

"We were doing just that," Jenny interrupted, "when we got caught. We're not stepping another foot into Chinatown. It'd be like walking right back in the lion's den."

Andi agreed. "We plan to hide Lin Mei and Kum Ju at my aunt's until I can talk to my brother. He's a lawyer. He'll know what to do."

"What if I take the little slaves to the Home?" Freddie offered. "I know where it is. I know the lady who runs the place. Won't take long and—"

"No!" shrieked Lin Mei. She and Kum Ju had settled themselves to the sidewalk in front of the restaurant. Obviously Lin Mei had been listening to every English word. She sprang from her spot and clutched Andi's skirt. "No leave missee. No go to white devil house without missee."

"I reckon that's your answer," Jenny said. "We've had a time convincing them to go at all. So, like Andi said, could you please point out which of these blamed hills we need to climb to get to Pacific Heights?"

"Suit yourself," Freddie said. "Wait here." He darted into a narrow alley next to the restaurant. When he returned he was leading a frisky sorrel horse. It tossed its head and pranced lightly behind Freddie. "He's a mite green and unpredictable, but he's got heart," he said. "He'll save you a long walk—if you can ride him."

Speechless, Andi stared at this generous gift. The two miles up the hills of the city suddenly seemed like a stroll in the park, and all because of the kindness of a stranger. She reached out and stroked the sorrel's flank. "I don't know what to say."

"Say thank you and let's go," Jenny said. She held out her hand to Freddie. "You, sir, are a gentleman, and I thank you kindly."

Freddie blushed and shook Jenny's hand. "No need t' thank me. I'm a sucker for a couple of pretty girls in a fix." Quickly he boosted Andi onto the horse's back. She grabbed the reins and steadied the lively animal with a few quiet words.

Freddie smiled up at her. "You'll do." He helped Jenny up and gently set Lin Mei and Kum Ju between the two older girls. "The fog's burned off, so you shouldn't have any trouble seeing your way. This here's Union. If you follow it far enough, you'll end up where you need to be."

"I'm sure I can find the house once I'm on Pacific Heights. I know the name of the street," Andi said. She reached down and took his hand. "Thank you again, Freddie. I don't know what we'd have done without your help. And lending us your horse"—she shook her head—"not many folks would trust their horse to a stranger. We'll bring him back, and we'll pay you for the loan of him too." She sat up and gathered the reins to leave.

Freddie laughed. "No need. He ain't my horse. I snitched him from the livery around back." With that, he gave the animal a smack on the rear.

The sorrel took off like a shot. Lin Mei and Kum Ju shrieked in terror. Andi couldn't breathe from the little girl's grip around her waist. But oh, how good it felt to be riding astride a young, spirited horse! She wished she could give him his head all the way to Aunt Rebecca's. The sorrel sensed her delight and snorted his pleasure at the morning ride. His four young riders didn't seem to burden him in the least.

Andi felt Lin Mei slip. "Easy, fella," she told the horse, and reined him in to a more leisurely pace—one that wouldn't frighten his riders. With a happy sigh, Andi knew it wouldn't be long before they left the lower city far behind.

"It's not very funny what Freddie did," Jenny said as they turned onto a familiar street a half hour later. "We're horse thieves now."

Andi's spirits were soaring—she could see Aunt Rebecca's mansion only a block away. "Aw, don't fret about that. Justin'll take care of it. I'm more worried about getting into the yard unseen. We have to use the gate."

Jenny squinted at the bright, mid-morning sun. "Oh, swell. It's broad daylight, and no fog in sight."

Andi knew it would be tricky. They'd originally planned to sneak in under the cover of dusk. It was still possible, however, to slip past the large front windows. Aunt Rebecca was probably lingering over her breakfast coffee in the dining room, which sat on the far side of the house. "We'll tie up the horse and creep around back as quick as we can. I won't leave you for long—just until things simmer down and I get the chance to come for you."

Jenny gave a curt nod. "All right, I'll have a go, but I'm tired of sneaking around and hiding."

Andi nudged the sorrel, and he broke into a trot. Her heart was bursting with joy and relief. They'd done it! They'd rescued Lin Mei and Kum Ju from a terrible life of slavery. In a few days, the little girls would be safe in the mission home, where they'd be loved and cared for.

Happily immersed in her thoughts, she didn't notice anything out of the ordinary until Jenny remarked, "There's sure a lot of horses and rigs tied up in front of your aunt's house. You don't suppose . . . ?"

Andi yanked the horse to a stop and gasped. "I should have known the police would come here!"

The door to Aunt Rebecca's flew open. Several people clattered down the steps toward them, including four uniformed policemen.

In a moment, she and her friends were surrounded.

## Chapter Eighteen

# "Go with Gladness"

Andi reacted instantly. *Ride far and fast!* She dug her heels into the sorrel's flank, but a figure in dark blue snatched the bridle and hung on. Hot tears sprang to her eyes. The policemen would not, *could* not capture Lin Mei and Kum Ju. She tried once more to make the horse leap forward.

"None of that, missy," a deep, Irish voice commanded. Strong arms circled her waist and pulled her from the horse. "You've given San Francisco's finest a merry chase. I'll not be havin' you run off just when you've been found."

Andi shut her ears to the policeman's words. She turned into a fighting, biting wildcat, intent on clawing her way out from the man's strong grip. She'd been held against her will once too often, and this brute would pay. "Let me go!"

To her surprise, the policeman released her. Andi stumbled against the horse, breathing hard. She looked up, and was instantly engulfed in a warm, tight embrace.

"Take it easy, honey," Justin said, holding her close. "Sergeant O'Malley's only trying to help."

Andi clung to her brother. "Don't let the police take them back, Justin. Let them stay here, at least a few days. They've been treated so cruelly. Please make Aunt Rebecca understand. You're a . . . you're a . . . lawyer. You . . ." She choked on her words and broke into sobs.

Aunt Rebecca elbowed her way forward. There were tears in her eyes. "My dear child," she murmured, placing a gentle hand on Andi's head, "what a sorry sight you are. Don't make yourself ill. Of course

131

they may stay. Whatever gave you the idea that I wouldn't welcome these waifs into my home, once I knew of their plight?"

Andi lifted her head from Justin's chest and blinked back tears. "B-but, Auntie, you were making me come home because of what happened at the school. I figured you were cross because I wasn't behaving properly—that I was mucking up the Carter name and your reputation by associating with . . ." She paused at the stricken look on her aunt's face.

Rebecca raised a handkerchief to wipe her eyes. "Stuff and non-sense! I expect certain behavior from polite society, and I hold my family to the highest standard. However, there is also the matter of Christian charity. These should go hand in hand, but if they clash on occasion"—she looked up at the motionless girls on horseback—"then by all means, the Higher Law must prevail." She sighed. "You should have told me, Andrea, instead of hiding the child and then traipsing off to Chinatown without so much as a by-your-leave." She waved her handkerchief like a fan before her face. "Chinatown. The very idea!"

"I agree," Justin said. He held Andi at arm's length and frowned. "You gave us quite a fright. We pieced together what happened from Juan Carlos and from Miss Whitaker, who notified the police as soon as she learned you were missing. They scoured Chinatown all night, looking for you and your friends, but you'd disappeared without a trace." He gripped her shoulders and gave her a gentle shake. "Do you have any idea where you might have ended up?"

Andi looked at the ground. She knew all too well. "Yes, sir," she said in a small voice, "I do know. And I'm sorry." She raised her head. "But it wasn't wrong to want to help Lin Mei and Kum Ju. I never planned to go into Chinatown, but the mission home was closer, and it seemed like the better choice."

Justin was nodding. "I know." He pulled her into another heartfelt hug. "Just so you're safe. That's all that matters."

"What's going to happen now?" She peeked around Justin and saw her sister Kate and the kids behind Aunt Rebecca.

Levi waved. "Howdy, Andi. Don't you know nuthin' about the city? You should've took me along."

Andi didn't reply. She searched Justin's face for an answer to her question.

He sighed. "Until we sort everything out, your friends can stay here." He indicated the policemen. "These gentlemen are part of the Chinatown Squad. They know what goes on there. They won't tell anyone. Your secret is safe for the time being."

"Yippee!" Jenny crowed. She slid from the horse and helped Lin Mei and Kum Ju to the ground. "I know you'll think of something, Mr. Carter. Andi told me you're a smart lawyer and know all the tricks. Glad to meet you."

"And it's a pleasure to meet you, Miss . . . ?" He held out his hand.

Jenny clasped Justin's hand and pumped it. "Jenny. Jenny Grant. And I'm mighty glad you're here. Andi said you could smooth the ruffled feathers on her Aunt Reb—"

"Jenny!" Andi gasped. She felt her face flame. Rebecca clucked her tongue disapprovingly.

Justin laughed. "Never mind. Let's go inside, where you ladies can rest, clean up, eat, and tell us your story."

Aunt Rebecca, whose "ruffled feathers" were rustling at Jenny's remark, nodded. "I'll have the maid draw you girls a bath first thing."

Andi watched her aunt disappear into the house. "I never thought Aunt Rebecca would allow Lin Mei and Kum Ju to stay here. She's always fretting about how things look and what people may think."

"You don't know our aunt as well as you think you do," Justin remarked. "She's a blustery old woman who believes she knows best, but she has principles. She told me that if she'd even suspected the little Chinese girl in the school's kitchen was a slave, she would have rescued the child herself."

Andi's mouth fell open. "Auntie said that?"

He nodded. "She's been worried half to death over you. She hasn't slept all night." Then he grinned. "But never fear. I'm sure Aunt Rebecca will be back to her normal, bossy self by the end of the week." He winked. "Come on, honey, let's get you and your friends settled."

As promised, Justin took care of everything, even the stolen horse. Andi had no idea her oldest brother knew so many important people in San Francisco.

"It's all arranged," he announced at the end of luncheon a week later. It was a quiet, private meal with Andi, Aunt Rebecca, Jenny, and the Chinese girls. He smiled across the white linen tablecloth at Lin Mei and Kum Ju. They looked like different children from the frightened and browbeaten girls Andi and Jenny had rescued. Their eyes were bright, and their faces glowed with happiness. They were giggling and playing Cat's Cradle together while Justin spoke. "This afternoon I'll accompany these two cheerful ladies to the mission home. Miss Culbertson is more than happy to receive them. She has temporary guardianship until the hearing."

Lin Mei looked up at his words. "I go with gladness. Learn of Jesus-God. He make my heart happy." She turned to Kum Ju and spoke a few words in Chinese. Kum Ju nodded and whispered in Lin Mei's ear. Lin Mei smiled. "Kum Ju say Jesus-God make her heart happy, too. "

"Indeed He does." Then Justin turned sober. "I've been through enough of these hearings to realize there are no guarantees in court. If I had a nickel for every time a Chinese came forward and claimed a relationship to one of these little slave girls, I'd be a rich man."

"You *are* a rich man," Jenny piped up.

Justin grinned. "There. You see? Seriously, ladies, I promise I'll do my best to see that Lin Mei and Kum Ju are allowed to remain at the mission. You can pray to that end."

"Maybe nasty old Feng Chee will think twice about going after Lin Mei, now that it's been proven she didn't steal the jewels," Andi said.

She giggled. "I wish I'd been there to see the look on Miss Whitaker's face when the police found her jewelry case stuffed into a hidey hole behind the cook stove."

"We missed all the fun," Jenny agreed with a sigh. "Watching Feng Chee scuttle away after it came out that he lied would have been a pure treat for me."

Justin chuckled. "I'm sorry you girls had to miss it. I admit I felt a certain satisfaction watching Feng Chee unsuccessfully try to worm his way out of his guilt."

"I bet Miss Whitaker scorched his ears good before she sent him and his wife packing," Andi added with a grin. "She sure knows how to give a scolding."

"Andrea, please," Aunt Rebecca said from the end of the table, "Miss Whitaker is a fine woman and a good headmistress. This has been a trying week for her. I insist you speak respectfully."

"Yes, ma'am."

Andi and Jenny exchanged satisfied looks. Feng Chee and his wife no longer worked at the school, and Juan Carlos had assured Andi that *Señor* Hunter's memory of the events in the stable was fuzzy. *That crack on his head must have been a good one.* Andi hoped Mr. Hunter's memory remained fuzzy for a long time.

Justin rose from the table. "I'll take the little girls to Miss Culbertson and be back in time to catch the afternoon ferry to Oakland. Andi, pack your things and be ready to go when I return."

"Why? Where are we going?"

"Back to the ranch, of course. You've had quite a time in the city, and I'm sure Mother will understand if I take you home a few weeks early."

"Mr. Carter!" Jenny was on her feet in a flash. "You can't take Andi home."

Before Justin could reply, Aunt Rebecca spoke up.

"Justin, you're not serious."

"Perfectly serious." He turned to Andi. "Would you like to go home?"

Andi looked around the table. She wanted to go back to the ranch and Taffy, but how could she say good-bye to her new friends now? She heard the shrill laughter of Levi and Betsy from the next room and realized she hadn't spent much time with her nieces and nephew either. And, of course, she wanted to be in the city when Justin came back for the hearing for Lin Mei and Kum Ju.

She took a deep breath and said, "I'll stay."

To find out more about Andi and Taffy, and even get your questions answered, log on to www.homeschoolblogger.com/CircleCRanch/. To read more about Susan K. Marlow's adventures or to contact her, e-mail susankmarlow@kregel.com.

# HISTORICAL NOTE

Although this story is fiction, the sad plight of thousands of Chinese girls in the late 1800s in California, especially San Francisco, was real. Many were sold by their desperately poor parents in Canton, China, for less than forty dollars, or kidnapped and hidden aboard ships bound for the Golden Mountain (America). Once in port, the girls were smuggled into San Francisco, or worse—allowed through immigration by bribed officials who looked the other way. The Chinese slave traders pretended to be the girls' relatives and presented false papers, then spirited the girls away to Chinatown.

Little girls—some no more than six or seven years old—carried their owners' babies on their backs while cleaning, cooking, and doing the family's laundry. Others chopped wood or sewed for hours on end. They suffered terrible abuse from cruel masters and mistresses.

This so-called "yellow slave trade" spurred Margaret Culbertson and Donaldina Cameron* to courageously mount rescue operations into the heart of Chinatown. Their work is credited with saving more than three thousand Chinese girls from hopeless bondage. The Occidental Mission Home for Girls, begun in 1874, stood as a bold fortress on the edge of Chinatown, caring for the physical and spiritual needs of these rescued "Children of Darkness."

For forty years, God protected *Lo-Mo* (Miss Cameron's Chinese name, which means "Old Mother") during her daring raids. The

---

*Margaret Culbertson's successor who came to the Home in 1895 and stayed forty years.

rescued girls thrived in the Home, surrounded by the love and care of Christian missionaries. Many former slaves received the gospel of Christ's love and grew up to become respected citizens, wives, and mothers. Some went to college and returned to their native Canton to help put a stop to the evil trade.

The Occidental Mission Home still stands at 920 Sacramento Street in San Francisco's Chinatown. It is renamed the Donaldina Cameron House, in honor of Donaldina and her tireless work on behalf of the Chinese people. Today the Cameron House is a multiservice agency serving individuals, immigrant families, and youth in Asian communities of the San Francisco Bay area.

To learn more about the Donaldina Cameron House, go to: http://www.cameronhouse.org/history.htm.

## Circle C Adventures Book 1

# ANDREA CARTER AND THE LONG RIDE HOME

Twelve-year-old Andi Carter can't seem to stay out of trouble. Now her beloved horse, Taffy, is missing and it's Andi's fault. The daring young girl will do anything to find the thief and recover Taffy. But her choices plunge her into danger, and Andi discovers that life on her own in the Old West can be downright terrifying!

*Circle C Adventures Book 2*

# ANDREA CARTER AND THE
# DANGEROUS DECISION

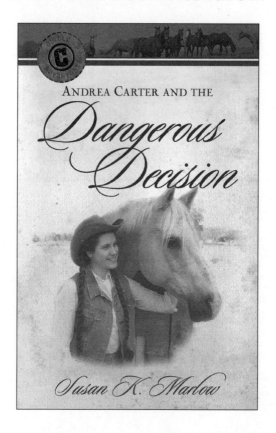

Andi nearly tramples her new teacher in a reckless, impromptu horse race down the main street of Fresno, California—not a good way to begin the fall school term. Her troubles multiply when she must decide if she should deliberately walk into a dangerous situation to rescue the teacher's mean-spirited, troublemaking daughter.

## Circle C Adventures Book 3

# ANDREA CARTER AND THE FAMILY SECRET

Why had Andi never been told the secret her family has carefully kept hidden? Angry and hurt at being left out, Andi saddles Taffy and sets out to find some answers—answers that turn her world upside down. How far must Andi go to rescue those she loves and whose lives depend on her protection?